Book Four, Broken

Fated Saga Fantasy Series

Rachel Humphrey - D'aigle

ISBN 978-1467992633

Cover Photograph by Danielle Page Photography

http://www.daniellepagephotography.com/

BROKEN

Chapter One

Meghan Jacoby stepped over the hillside and walked down to the open field below. The cool autumn breeze, which she normally would have relished, whisked through her flame red hair unnoticed.

Her target walked toward her, unknowingly into a trap. As he drew near, she forced herself to smile.

Meghan was surprised when her welcome turned from fake to real, as she could not help but race the last remaining steps and throw her arms around the brother she had not seen for months. All her fear and anxiety momentarily dissipated.

He returned the gesture, holding her tight.

"I've missed you so much Colin," she admitted in a whisper, attempting to forget why she was here.

He hugged her deeper.

Meghan's relief at seeing him alive and well turned sour, as her task could not be buried away; but she did successfully keep her thoughts hidden from him.

"I am sorry, Sis," Colin said. "But you know I couldn't take the chance. In the end, it's better for us to stay in hiding." He released his grip, sighed, and closed his eyes, taking a calming breath.

"Are you okay?" Meghan asked him, at once thinking how ironic her question was, considering the reason for their visit. She kept her thoughts firmly blocked, so as not to betray her cause.

"Yes, I'm fine," he answered, opening his eyes. "Can you believe where life has taken us, Meghan? Could you ever have imagined this?"

"No. Not even in a hundred years could I have imagined this," she replied with a slight chuckle. "It's a long way from our travels with Uncle Arnon." *No. Imagining what I'm about to do is not something I could have thought up ever, even in my wildest dreams.* She hung tight to the thought, keeping it securely locked in her own mind.

Meghan desired greatly to flee from her current path, but knew that was not an option. "How is Catrina?" she asked, trying not to arouse suspicion.

"Um. She's..."

Meghan panicked when he did not answer right away. Did he suspect something?

Colin twisted his face before finally answering. "I was hoping to show you, actually."

"She's here!" said Meghan, not believing her fortune. She had been afraid they might never find Catrina after today. Instantly, Meghan regretted her thoughts.

To whose fortune was it that Catrina was here?

"Of course she's here," replied Colin. "She refuses to leave my side. And she puts up with a lot... I mean, I have killed her three times." He winked, knowing Meghan would understand his sick joke.

A moment later, a small body covered in a dark cloak popped out from behind Colin, embracing Meghan.

"I cannot tell you what it means for us to see you," cried Catrina, happily.

"Life is too short," replied Meghan, gasping at the ease of Catrina's welcome. "No matter what, you are my family, and I love you *both,* very much."

And that much was true. For all their flaws, she did honestly love them both. Colin, because he was and always would be her brother, and Catrina because Colin loved her.

Meghan's eyes filled with tears. She took a deep breath and bit her tongue, trying to retain her composure, and allowed Catrina to take her place by Colin's side.

She swallowed, hard, keeping her thoughts blocked. Meghan could sense Colin's attempts to penetrate them, and knew there was not much time to complete her mission. He would break into them soon.

"So, my darling husband, would you like to tell her our news, or should I?" Catrina said, grinning widely.

"News?" questioned Meghan.

Colin's eyes twinkled and he motioned for Catrina to share her secret. Meghan watched as she took off the bulky cloak.

"Be prepared for something to take you off guard," Ivan Crane had warned her, repeatedly, during their rehearsals for this confrontation. "It's bound to happen and you cannot lose control."

Ivan's warnings could not have prepared her for what she was now witnessing. Meghan's legs nearly faltered. "Catrina... you're ... you're pregnant!"

"Yes. Isn't it wonderful?"

Meghan lost her control. The calm place she had kept herself disappeared. Her breathing sped up and her hands shook.

"No. No. No," she muttered. Taking a step back, she glanced at her brother. "Oh, Colin, I didn't know."

All the planning and practice for this moment was for nothing!

Meghan, along with everyone involved, would die now.

She could not go through with it!

Meghan lost control of her mind-block and Colin easily penetrated her thoughts. His face contorted in confused anger.

"What! What!" he kept repeating. "How could you?" he demanded, stepping closer to his sister.

Meghan flinched, no longer able to contain her fear of the brother she had once thought it was her job to protect.

"I'm sorry," she insisted. "Oh, God, I really am. And I had no idea she was pregnant, Colin."

Catrina just stood like a statue, bewildered at what was happening.

The ground beneath Meghan's feet began to rumble as Colin's temper flared; his eyes turned to blood red, indicating he was losing control as well. His fists balled up tightly, and he rocked back and forth.

"Why are you people always trying to kill us?" he shouted angrily. "When will you learn that you'd all be better off if you just left us alone?" He paused, adding, "I'm going to send you away, Catrina. I don't want you to get hurt, again."

Catrina stepped forward to protest, and before Colin could act, Meghan withdrew a long silver blade and lunged at her brother.

Out of instinct, to save the man she loved, Catrina leapt in the way. The knife plunged directly into her heart.

Death was quick.

But her eyes begged to know why as she took her final breath.

It was what they had hoped for, Meghan and Ivan. In all their planning, *this* was the best scenario: for Catrina to offer her life to save Colin's.

Meghan withdrew the dagger, bewildered at what she had done.

Breathe, she reminded herself. *The job is not finished yet!*

Colin, in angst of seeing his beloved wife Catrina slump to the ground fell to her side, and although clearly furious over the act, he did not look worried in the least over her death.

Meghan was prepared as a magical barrier materialized around both he and Meghan, blocking anything or anyone else from getting in, or out.

She had expected this, too.

Just the two of them.

No one else.

Meghan shook, unable to calm herself, as she prepared for what she had to do next.

At first, Colin just stared at Catrina's lifeless body. He touched her swollen belly, laying his head on it, as if to listen. Everything had changed after she had taken over Colin's life. There was no more Colin Jacoby. She was Colin's life, completely and unconditionally; one could not exist without the other. And for that unconditional love, they would both have to pay the ultimate price.

It was unfair. Meghan had said it many times. Unfair that her brother and the woman he loved were cursed by a power they never asked for, and could not control.

Meghan still held the bloody knife that had taken Catrina's life. She could barely catch her breath, and questioned whether she could go through with the final part. But if she didn't act while Colin was still distracted, it would be too late!

Outside the magical barrier, Meghan saw the entire Svoda army, lead by Ivan Crane, rise up over the hillside. Plan B, should she fail. However, if she failed, everyone on that hill would die, including Ivan.

Nona, Meghan's loyal Catawitch, stood at Ivan's feet, anxious to be back by Meghan's side.

"Do it now!" said Ivan, through Nona's thoughts to Meghan. "You must!"

Tears flowed freely down Meghan Jacoby's face. Maybe Colin would take her life and end the torment she knew would follow if she survived.

Colin stood up, facing Meghan.

Ivan and Nona could tell Meghan was losing her nerve.

"Remember!" Ivan told her.

Meghan nodded.

Colin laughed.

"Never in *my* wildest dreams did I think this day would come, and it would be you and Ivan Crane working together. They cannot touch me in here, you know. But don't worry, Sis," he said, moving closer. "I'll take care of them when I'm through with you."

"I don't know what to say, Colin. I am sorry, but I have no choice." Her voice was shaky but truthful.

"No choice," he mocked. "And what exactly are you going to do to me, Sister? You never were any good at magic," he chastised.

He was no longer the Colin Jacoby she had grown up with. No longer the Colin Jacoby she used to protect from bullies. And no longer the Colin Jacoby she had once shared her most intimate thoughts, fears and dreams with. He had been changed, and all because he loved Catrina. Their love had blinded him to all else.

Meghan looked away from Colin, ready for what was inevitably to come.

The pain came, searing through her veins like a knife. She doubled over, unable even to scream.

"Stop this Colin!" demanded Ivan.

Colin snapped his head in Ivan's direction and he instantly fell to the same fate as Meghan, dropping to the ground, writhing in agony.

No one dared touch him.

Meghan's pain subsided, but she saw that Ivan's did not.

"Forget about me," Ivan mustered out.

Meghan looked away, still crouched and looking at the ground.

"You can't kill me, Meghan. I know you too well. You always thought you were the strong one, the brave one, the daring one who could do whatever it took to survive. Turns out you were the weak one, after all," he said hatefully.

"Whatever you say, Colin. I don't have any fight left in me," she lied. "I'm sorry I killed her, but as I said, I have no other choice." Meghan voice wavered at the end and she kept her eyes on the ground. She could not face him.

"Why would you even attempt taking her from me?" he questioned. "You know it is a pointless endeavor."

Meghan could not answer. Her heart was beating so hard she felt sure it would burst through her skin.

"Look at me!" Colin demanded with such fury that she instantly looked up, seeing his betrayed eyes. He invaded her mind, easily listening to her confused thoughts ... *You're not my brother any more ... I can't believe I killed her... I can't do it... Don't give up... Too many have already suffered... You know what has to be done! Do it!*

Colin's stare turned deadly.

The horrific pain returned and Meghan fell to the ground, unable to move or breathe, but her grip remained tight around the bloodied silver blade. She did not know how much longer she would live, but she had to finish her mission.

Then, Colin's anger diminished, as he appeared to inwardly struggle with the idea of killing his own sister. The pain stopped again, but Meghan's hope was premature. Colin leaned over her, staring into her eyes.

"I believe I'll bring Catrina back now, so she can watch me avenge her death. She loved you like a sister, you know. I think you at least owe her an apology before I kill you."

The struggle Meghan thought she had seen in him was not there.

"Even you, Colin Jacoby," Meghan said boldly, "cannot bring back the dead, who have given their life to save another!" She paused, letting the statement sink in. "Catrina knowingly sacrificed her life so you could live."

Colin looked down to his beloved.

Could this be true?

Sacrifice was not reversible.

"I don't believe you."

"Then try it. Bring her back!"

Colin glared, but bent over his wife's limp body. In his mind be pictured her alive and at his side.

No breath.

No movement.

"What is this?" Colin asked. "Live!" he ordered Catrina's still body.

A fury was about to be unleashed, the likes of which no one had ever witnessed, unless Meghan acted now. She could not, and would not, allow everyone she cared about to suffer any longer.

With a pained cry, Meghan jumped off the ground and plunged the dagger into Colin's back and through his heart. One fatal wound, from which he could not recover.

She felt his shock and pain and cried out with him.

Memories flooded her mind, ones they shared, as children, and new ones she had never seen before.

Meghan wondered briefly, if in her moment of death, this is what it would feel like. She stored the rush of memories, the good and the bad... it was the least she could do for the brother she loved so dearly.

She let go of the knife, leaving it in her brothers back.

He slumped onto the ground, next to the still Catrina and her unborn child.

Colin Jacoby was dead.

Killed by the hands of his sister and once protector.

He was no longer present in Meghan's mind. She had never wanted to experience it again... his absence, and the emptiness it left behind.

This time, it was for good. He would not return.

She would never again hear his thoughts or be comforted by his presence.

The magical barrier which Colin had created vanished with his final breath, and Ivan and Nona rushed to Meghan's side.

No cheers resounded in the field of victory.

Only whimpers over the lives that had to be ended.

Ivan Crane held Meghan Jacoby close. "You did what had to be done," he repeated to her.

Nona rubbed her face against Meghan's, but did not feel her there.

She could not breathe.

She could not see.

She had committed the ultimate betrayal.

She may have destroyed the evil that had taken control of the world, but that evil had taken control of *her* brother.

"She was pregnant, Ivan," Meghan choked out. "We killed an innocent child."

"It is regretful," he whispered, taking her head into his hands. Looking Meghan in the eye, he added, "They hid that secret well, but it changed nothing. Had we allowed that child to be born, it would have suffered the same fate."

Meghan knew Ivan was right. Why did he always have to be right?

"We both knew you were the only one who could ever get close enough, Meghan. I am just so sorry it had to be you. If I could have done it for you …" he did not finish.

The realization of the lives she had taken was more than Meghan could bear. Her tears turned to sobs. She fell to her knees, her mind reaching out for the brother that could no longer hear her.

Ivan kept his arms wrapped around her, knowing there was nothing he could say to ease her pain. After a minute, he helped her stand.

The Svoda army stood behind, unsure of what to do next. No one could say or do anything to take away Meghan Jacoby's pain.

Meghan closed her eyes, not wishing to see Colin and Catrina Jacoby's lifeless bodies, but she could not forget. Her mind's eye saw the knife stabbing them, over and over again. Her head grew dizzy and at that moment, her body gave out.

Ivan Crane swiped her into his arms, gently kissing her forehead, and then carried her away from the memories he knew she would never forget.

A flame flickered, casting a woman's silhouette against a cave wall.

"This is a future I cannot allow to happen," she whispered to the shadows.

After the candle of the daughter she had believed dead had lit months before, she had intensely desired to have a vision of her daughter's future. However, the vision she had just witnessed was devastating, and her heart felt heavy with the weight of it. She leapt to her feet, dashing through the rows of lit candles, searching for one in the shape of a young man. She found it and knelt down on the cold ground.

"I will not allow this future to take place. I've changed it before, I'll change it again!" she spat out determinedly. "But if I am to succeed at changing this future I will need help."

She peered into the flames, whispering. "Hear me, child."

The young man in the flame lay sleeping in a bed. He stirred, but did not wake.

"Hear me," she repeated. "You must find me."

The young man replied, while yet asleep. "Where must I go?"

"When you awake, you will know where to find me."

"Why must I find you?" the boy asked.

"Because I can show you, Sebastien Jendaya, how to save the ones you lost and love."

Sebastien did not answer. His eyes darted back and forth under closed eyelids, dreaming vividly of a vast forest leading to the entrance of a cave.

Chapter Two

"We have been walking for an hour," said Meghan Jacoby, nearly dropping her bags from exhaustion.

"Yes, I know," replied her brother, Colin. "I've been listening to you complain about it the entire time."

Meghan retorted by sticking out her tongue.

She walked alongside Colin near the back of the caravan, as they headed toward their new home, both glad to be out of Limbo after narrowly escaping from Eidolon's Valley, and the clutches of the now deceased Goblin King (a fact only Colin and his hidden dream girl, Catrina Flummer knew).

Colin could *not* escape the inevitable questions and stares that followed the Svoda learning that he, a magical newcomer, had killed a Scratcher. A feat never accomplished before even by the most powerful of the Svoda Gypsies.

Having Catrina securely behind him gave him strength to continue; rescuing her was worth every awed and incredulous stare.

Ivan Crane stepped cautiously a few steps behind them. Although he could not see Catrina at Colin's side, he knew she was there and appeared reluctant to allow too much distance between them. Meghan, as well as Colin, knew Ivan well enough to know how badly he wanted Catrina to tell him everything she knew about his mother.

"We're almost there now," they all heard someone announce, up ahead. Many sighs of relief echoed through the weary travelers, many of whom still nursed injuries from the battle with Eidolon.

The caravan stepped out of the dark forest they had journeyed through and into a bright meadow that glistened with a cover of recently fallen rain. Everyone stopped, temporarily blinded by the brightness. It took a moment for their eyes to adjust, and as each member regained clear visibility, no one moved. Instead, they waited with baited breath, each staring in speechless dread at an unexpected sight.

Fire had swept through the meadow, leaving behind only remnants of the huts that should have been their new homes. Smoke still smoldered on the wet ground. Belongings from the previous tenants lay strewn about the meadow, as if someone had been searching for something. At the same time indicating that the people living in the huts had either no chance of escape, or had made such a hasty retreat they had left everything behind.

Juliska Nandalia Blackwell, Banon (leader and Queen) of the Svoda Gypsies, took a few steps forward, followed by her personal Balaton, Jelen and Jenner Wandrer. They were brutish looking men, and also brothers.

"Everyone, stay here," she ordered softly, in as much disbelief and concern as the rest of the group.

"Could this be a trap?" asked Jelen, as she stepped into the meadow.

"I don't know," she answered truthfully. "You two, check the perimeter. Once we know its safe we will allow the rest to enter."

Her personal Balaton left her side and examined the entire meadow. There was no sign of a trap. Or life. Or anything that indicated what had occurred in the meadow, other than destruction.

Juliska motioned for the caravan to follow her. The Svoda remained silent, in awe of the devastation that lay before them, growing more fearful with each step.

Meghan left Colin's side to follow Ivan. She assumed he would be following Juliska. Colin stayed in the back of the group, behind the Mochrie family, with Catrina, still invisible by his side.

Suddenly a woman cried out in angst, shaking the rest of the group into life. The woman ran to a muddy blanket lying, still folded, on the ground. She grasped it in her hands, falling onto her knees.

"This blanket belongs to my daughter. I made it for her unborn child before we left our island."

The woman's statement confirmed the Svoda's worst fear: the belongings in the meadow belonged to another Svoda caravan.

"So where is everyone?" It was Billie Sadorus, who asked the question they were all thinking.

No one dared reply.

Cautiously, they stepped into the meadow, looking for any obvious clues. But the rest of the meadow held the same ominous scene: smoldering fire, strewn belongings, and no sign of life.

Juliska Blackwell swallowed hard and made an announcement.

"Initiated members, organize into your zones at once, we meet within the hour. Non-Initiated members, set up temporary living quarters away from the devastation." She paused, her face set in determination. "We will discover what has happened here. We will not leave until we do."

The caravan buzzed, nervously setting in to obeying their leader's orders. They searched their own belongings for tents and other camping supplies, setting up in the only corner of the meadow not covered in smoldering fires or haphazardly discarded belongings.

The Balaton set up a larger tent for zone meetings, which stood in between the tents for living in and the devastation in the meadow. In the center of their new living space, a cantina began to take shape.

Meghan and Colin helped the Mochries set up their tent, and were surprised at how fast the temporary tent city took shape. Exactly an hour later, all zone members headed for the large meeting tent, leaving everyone else to finish unpacking.

The meeting was surprisingly short. When it ended, everyone gathered in the cantina.

"The Viancourt will vote now," Ivan informed Meghan, Colin and Jae, upon seeing them.

"On what?" Jae asked him.

"We'll all find out soon," Ivan replied, not revealing anything discussed in the meeting.

A few minutes later, Pantin Hollee exited the tent, ready with an announcement.

"All zones leaders met and spoke their views, and the Viancourt has taken a vote and decided unanimously, that as of this moment, the following rules will be strictly enforced."

The meadow was silent as she spoke.

"No one is to leave this meadow without the direct permission of the Viancourt. A curfew is set for sunset, meaning you must all be in your tents by the time the sun is down, and no one shall use magic unless instructed by the Viancourt to do so!" she paused, taking a breath.

"The Balaton," she continued, "are setting up special measures, which will track any and all magic that has been, or is used, in this meadow. Anyone discovered using magic will be considered as interfering with this investigation, and will be promptly and severely punished!"

Pantin Hollee paused again.

"These rules are necessary if we are to discover the terrible truth about what has taken place here."

The group shouted their agreement. These rules seemed a small price to pay for the answers they all desperately wanted.

"Now disperse," added Pantin Hollee. "Tomorrow at first light, all zone leaders will attend a mandatory meeting to discuss further developments and plans. Until then, keep your eyes and ears open, and most of all, be safe."

##

Colby and his Catawitch, Elisha, trudged up a steep hill. At the top of the hill stood two trees, the trunks of which were tall and straight, but whose branches entwined around each other, like a gated entrance. The corner of Colby's mouth turned up slightly. His bright blue eyes peered sideways at Elisha.

"You know what to do," he said.

His Catawitch took out her front right paw and extended a claw, scratching Colby's hand. He winced only slightly, allowing the blood to pool in his palm. He stood in between the two trees, allowing the blood to pour out of his palm and onto the ground.

The instant it hit the ground a voice echoed.

"Welcome home young master. Your blood is true and you may enter."

Elisha jumped into Colby's arms and began licking his wounded hand.

"Terrible! Vile! Appalling!" she cattishly admonished. "Requiring a blood sacrifice every time you come home."

"Father has to be sure it's really me, Elisha. You know this."

"Still, it's cruel that I have to hurt my master each time he comes home."

"But I've got you to heal me, don't I?" he reminded her.

Elisha had already healed his wounded hand, using her Catawitch magic to do so. She jumped down, parading alongside him.

They no longer stood atop a lonely hill, but rather at the entrance of a vast estate. Colby stepped onto the cobblestone driveway, soon crossing a small wooden bridge. A stream trickled underneath, feeding the surrounding lush gardens with water.

"Ah, welcome home Young Master Colby," a voice spoke just after he crossed the bridge. Colby turned to see an older man sitting on an upside down bucket, with his gloved hands elbow deep into another steaming bucket. The foul stench quickly found Colby's nose.

"I'll never understand my father's love of gardens," he said.

The man got up off his bucket and leisurely made his way toward Colby. Manure still covered his elbow length gloves.

"Your father has good taste, Young Master. Knows good food when he's had it! Would you want to live off that stuff the others call food? Where they got the idea to use magic to grow their food I'll never figure out! Only had to try it once to see just how clearly using magic to grow food is about as idiotic as digging a water well in a sandbox! Nope. I'll be your father's gardener till my death, and happy to do it." He went back to his smelly, steaming bucket and left Colby to his own business.

Colby did not give any more thought to the matter. He had news to share with his father. News he hoped would please his father immensely.

Then his father appeared, standing in front of him at the entrance to the main house. His father's aged and gaunt face made no change at the sight of his son. He and Colby looked like ants standing in front of the house, which towered well above the tree line.

"Hello father," said Colby. "I have news."

Jurekai Fazendiin, the unspoken ruler of the immortal Grosvenor, motioned for his son to follow him, but said nothing.

Colby knew the drill well. He followed his father down a long corridor, knowing he would not speak of business until in the one room he knew with absolute certainty was safe for business conversations.

The long corridor opened to an oval room with ceilings a good thirty feet above Colby's head. The room and walls were bare, except for a stained glass portrait. Fazendiin stared fondly at the woman portrayed in the stained glass. She was dark haired, pale skinned, and her head tilted to one side, leaning against a pillow, sleeping.

"Wake up mother," asked Fazendiin gently.

Light emanated through the window, and the woman opened her eyes. She sat up, looking stern, nodding slightly at her son. She noted Colby standing a few feet away.

"My grandson, home at last," she spoke, understanding their appearance before her. Fazendiin knelt to the floor. Colby repeated his father's actions.

"I swear vengeance upon those that have done this to you, Mother! One day I will find a way to free your soul." Fazendiin then arose.

Colby followed.

"I know that one day you will fulfill your promise, my son. Now enter." She outstretched her arms as an orange and gold light shined forth from her body. Fazendiin stepped into the light, followed by his son.

They stood inside an oval, fire lit room. There were two chairs sitting on each side of the fireplace. Fazendiin sat in one of them, motioning for his son to sit in the other.

Colby, eager to announce his news, did not wait for his father to ask how his venture had gone. "The Svoda arrived at the destroyed camp earlier today, just as expected. They're definitely sticking around for awhile."

Fazendiin's voice was aged but acute as he replied.

"You have done well, Son. Soon, we will not only have our hands on the Magicante, but the Projector as well!"

Colby beamed. A happy father was a good thing indeed. However, Colby's happiness was short-lived.

"Now that the plan is in motion, I believe it is time to let the others play it out. You have been absent from your schooling for too long now."

This was unexpected. Colby had hoped that once he had proven his usefulness to his father, that school would be indefinitely postponed, if not permanently canceled.

"Father, couldn't I just finish this one task? And then go back to school?" he pleaded.

Jurekai shook his head as he spoke. "You have done the hard part. The rest of this task will simply unfold. Finishing your schooling is just as vital as any task I have ever asked of you. I want you to be ready for your future, and there are things you have not yet learned."

Colby sighed. He knew no amount of pleading would change his father's mind. But back to school? He despised the thought of being stuck behind a desk and books. There had been a time when he had enjoyed school, but that was when his mother was allowed to teach him. She was gone now. He had not seen her in three years.

"I have found a new teacher for you," his father explained, interrupting Colby's thoughts. "I think you will like this one."

"Great," Colby replied with fake enthusiasm. With each new teacher, he was never sure whether to prepare to be relieved or petrified. His previous teacher had been impatient, mean and demanding, but mostly, she had smelled old and musty.

"Your new classes begin tomorrow morning. Nine a.m. sharp!"

"Yes Father," answered Colby.

It looked like his task, and any fun outside the estate, was finished for now.

##

Meghan Jacoby awoke, confused by her surroundings. Then she noticed Nona at her feet and the memories came flooding into her mind.

"You'd think after more than a year of being on the move, I'd be used to waking up in strange places."

Meghan lay on a cot inside a tent, alongside Jae and Mireya Mochrie.

Colin had opted not to sleep in the tent, but rather outside, underneath the stars. Of course, she knew this had nothing to do with his desire to sleep outdoors, but only do to with Catrina Flummer. Sharing a room with three others, one of which didn't know anything about Catrina, made him uncomfortable. Therefore, he opted to sleep outside where he could speak to Catrina whenever the coast was clear.

Meghan's body begged her to return to slumber, but outside the tent, footsteps already bustled across the meadow, and voices echoed into the tent boosting her curiosity.

The noise awoke Jae and Mireya as well.

Meghan sighed, pushing off her blanket. There was no need to dress, as she had not bothered to undress the night before.

"Morning guys," she muttered sleepily.

Mireya answered back and then scurried out of the room, asking her mother if she needed any help. Meghan overheard but did not listen for the reply.

Jae sat on the edge of his bed, looking as tired as Meghan felt.

"So Jae, will we have any part to play in figuring out what happened to the other group?"

"Don't know actually," he answered sleepily. "I assume they'll keep us busy doing something."

Whenever Meghan and Jae happened to be alone together, she could not help but try to prod him into talking; still hoping he might divulge whatever torment he was hiding, and finally put an end to the nightmarish visions she kept having about him.

"Creepy, isn't it?" she suddenly said with a shiver. "Finding out three months passed while we were in Limbo. It felt like three hours."

Jae perked up the littlest bit. "Especially since Banon Blackwell didn't even know about that," he added. He didn't expand on the subject and headed to the outer room.

Foiled again! She would have to try to talk to him again, later.

"Good, you're up," Sheila said upon seeing Jae. "Mireya and I are about to go help serve breakfast, and after that, I'll need you to keep watch on your sister while your father and I attend a zone meeting."

"Sure, mom. I got it."

She gave him a quick pat on the shoulder and a smile and then departed.

Meghan's stomach growled. "I always get so hungry when the weather is cooler," she complained.

"You know, I'm starving this morning, too. Maybe our bodies know we've got three months worth of eating to catch up on," Jae said, his mood brightening at the idea of gorging on food.

"Let's go before it gets too crowded," added Meghan, leaving the tent and stepping into the meadow. Again, she hoped he might continue talking to her but as soon as they stepped outside and started walking, Jae withdrew, looking contemplative.

The air was crisp and the sky gray.

There was already a line forming in the cantina. They saw Sheila and Mireya serving food alongside Billie Sadorus.

Fires still smoldered throughout the meadow, serving as a constant reminder of the eerie task ahead.

Meghan glanced around for Colin but did not see him. She searched in her mind for his thoughts and located him sitting behind a jutting rock, near the edge of the meadow.

"Morning Colin," she sent him, quickly adding, "Catrina too!"

"Join us once you get breakfast," Colin replied.

"So maybe you don't look like you're talking to yourself," Meghan joked.

"Very funny, Sis! And hey, grab a little something extra for Catrina. I think she needs to eat more."

"Okay. See you in a minute."

Meghan explained to Jae.

"I'll grab a little extra too," he offered.

As Meghan and Jae were about to hop into the back of the line, rushed footsteps hurried alongside them, pushing them out of the way and cutting in.

"Darcy," muttered Meghan.

"Dulcy," added Jae.

Daveena was not with them.

The duo pushed aside two other younger children, grabbed a plate of food, and then pushed their way out of the line. As they walked back by, they stopped.

"I don't wait in line behind ditch-witches," sneered Darcy.

She did not permit Dulcy to add what would surely have been a witty retort, and instead, shoved a piece of bread into Dulcy's mouth, motioning for her to follow.

Meghan and Jae grabbed their breakfast and tried to make a beeline for Colin, however, Meghan stopped when a woman stepped in her path, blocking her. It was the same woman who had discovered the blanket the previous day, upon entering the meadow.

"You're a Firemancer," the woman said as if to start a conversation. She added nothing more. Her tired eyes bored into Meghan's searching for the answer to a question she had not yet asked.

"Um, yes," Meghan finally spoke, unsure how else to respond.

"Can't you see what has happened here? Can't you tell me what has happened to my daughter?"

Meghan lost her breath.

"Please, tell me. I must know," the woman begged.

The crowd quieted, all eyes starring at Meghan. *Is this something I could see? Is this what is expected from a Firemancer?* Her thoughts overwhelmed her. Was everyone waiting for her to see something? Wouldn't they all be expecting this from Juliska? Their leader?

Jae came to her rescue. "You know that being a seer doesn't work like that. Besides, you know that if Meghan did see something it would be directly reported to Banon Blackwell."

This answer did not quench the woman's desire.

"Well why can't it work like that? I want to know what's happened to my daughter," her voice started to shake. "Why won't you just tell me?" she beseeched Meghan.

"I'm sorry," said Meghan, stepping back.

Just then, two members of the Balaton came running around the corner.

The woman began to cry.

"Let me take you to your husband," one of them said calmly.

"I just want to know," she sobbed.

He smiled understandingly and took hold of her, gently walking away from the cantina.

"Go back to whatever you were doing," the second Balaton ordered the onlookers, at the same time motioning for Meghan and Jae to wait.

"Sorry about that," he aimed toward Meghan. "Husband says she's been inconsolable all night."

"It's okay," Meghan stated. "She's upset."

"Don't think twice about it," he added with a wink. "Just let us handle it. Keeping the peace, that's what we do."

Meghan nodded.

The Balaton grabbed a slice of toast and darted around the corner of a nearby tent.

Meghan and Jae quickly joined Colin, and the invisible Catrina, taking refuge behind the rock at the edge of the meadow.

"What was that all about?" Colin asked.

"She wanted me to *see* for her, and tell her what happened to her daughter," Meghan told him.

"Can you do that?" he asked.

"I hadn't really thought about it. I don't know."

Meghan handed Colin her extra food, which was most of her plate. She had lost her appetite. Colin handed some to Catrina, insisting that she eat.

Meghan snapped her head, freezing her eyes on a spot just into the woods.

"What?" Colin asked.

Meghan relaxed her gaze. "Nothing, jumpy I guess. Thought I saw a shadow. There's nothing there though," she said, while nodding in the direction she had been looking.

Colin, Catrina and Jae each looked as well, but saw nothing.

"Not to change the subject, or reiterate points we already know," Jae said after a bit, "but be careful." He lowered his voice so only they could hear. "I think the Balaton are spying on people."

"I thought they weren't using magic," Colin noted, having seen the Balaton walking through the meadow, rather than popping in, as usual. He had hoped this would make it simpler to keep Catrina hidden.

"Not supposed to be, but times are crazy. I just wouldn't rule it out."

Colin nodded that he understood, sighing deeply. Seeing his concerned face, Catrina took hold of his hand and squeezed.

Just then, a leaf hit Meghan in the head and fell into her lap.

"Like I said," Jae spoke. "Always know how to find us."

Meghan picked up the leaf and read the message.

"Well I am outta here. Jul... The Banon would like to see me," she said.

"You can stop calling her Banon," smirked Jae. "You don't have to call her that on my account."

"Sorry, I was just trying to stay formal when I talk about her in public."

"Yeah, but she's your teacher now, too. I get it."

"In that case then, I'm off to see Juliska," she said.

Meghan swore she saw Colin and Catrina shudder from the corner of her eye as she walked away.

##

Meghan made her way through the smoldering meadow to the opposite side, where Juliska's tent had been raised, and as usual, she was guarded by Jelen and Jenner Wandrer. As Meghan arrived, Pantin Hollee came skirting out of the tent's entrance.

"Oh, good! You got the Banon's note. You can see yourself inside, she's waiting for you," said Hollee as she scurried away.

Before entering, Meghan wondered if she should say hello to Jelen and Jenner, but decided against it, seeing their stern faces keeping watch over the tent and the surrounding meadow and woods.

She had expected to step inside the tent and see a lavish space and setting, like the magical insides of the gypsy wagons, but instead the setting was intimate. The furnishings were sparse and simple: a long table with chairs, and a stove, which still threw off warmth even though the fire had clearly died, leaving behind just smoldering embers.

The tent had just two other rooms, both with closed canvas doors. Through the one on the right, Juliska's head popped out.

"Would you please join me in my room Meghan," she spoke, getting immediately down to business. "There is something I wish to discuss with you."

Meghan followed her into another sparsely furnished room, which included a bed covered in thick blankets, and three large travel trunks. One sat, closed, at the foot of her bed. The second was sitting on its side, and open, serving as a closet. The third was also on its side, and oddly, had two ornate doors inside. *That must be a magical space. Wonder what's in there?* As if to answer her question, Juliska stepped toward the trunk.

"The door on the right remains locked. However, the one on the left I believe you will find of great interest. But first, there is an urgent matter of which we must speak." She sat on the edge of her bed and motioned for Meghan to join her.

Meghan sat, facing Juliska, waiting eagerly for her to speak.

Juliska inhaled deeply, but said nothing. The longer the silence continued, the more Meghan's nerves fluttered, turning her thankfully empty stomach upside down.

Had the Balaton discovered Catrina? What would this mean for her brother? Her heart skipped, but she tried to keep a straight face as she waited for Juliska to speak.

"I am afraid…" the Banon began and stopped, swallowing hard.

This can't be good! Meghan's thoughts raced quickly, debating whether she should speak up first and admit that they had brought Catrina back with them, from Eidolon's Valley.

"I am afraid," began the Banon again, "that I have a difficult favor to ask of you, Meghan. But I would not ask unless I had exhausted all other options."

Meghan's heart slowed back to a normal rhythm for just a moment. This could not have anything to do with Catrina, or her brother.

"And I must stress that anything we discuss here in this room, is strictly between the two of us. No one else!"

Meghan's eyes were wide with curiosity now, and her heart once again quickened pace.

Juliska sighed. "I am completely freaking you out. I'm sorry, this was exactly what I wanted to avoid." She stood up and started pacing.

"This room is my safe room. Anything I say or do in here cannot be seen, overheard or witnessed by anyone not in this room. In addition, to enter, you must be invited by me. Few people have this honor."

Meghan nodded that she understood but could not find her voice to speak.

"I need your help, Meghan. The kind of help that only a Firemancer can offer. What I am about to tell you is a secret I have kept for many long months. Not even my loyal Pantin has been told."

Meghan felt her stomach lurch. What secret could Juliska possibly want to tell her, that she could not or would not tell another soul?

Juliska slid onto the bed and grasped Meghan's hands, inhaling deeply. Upon exhaling her secret slipped across her lips.

"I have not had a vision in over a year."

Meghan could think of no response.

"I do not know what has caused this, but my visions have simply vanished," Juliska continued. She let go of Meghan and started pacing the room again.

"I did not realize it was possible to lose them," Meghan whispered.

"Nor did I. It is a first, as far as my knowledge is aware. Perhaps this lifestyle is..." Juliska did not finish.

Meghan's thoughts filled in the blanks. *Stressful. Tiresome. Dangerous...*

"Regardless of the reason, Meghan, when I discovered you were a Firemancer, I knew instantly that I would come to rely on your visions if mine continued to fail me. I am afraid to admit I have been rather selfish in my cause. My lack of vision is why I pushed your training along so quickly. This is why I allowed you to be Ivan Crane's Learner Companion in Eidolon's Valley. I will point out, that I would not have pushed if I was not one hundred percent confident that you were up to the task!"

"I never feel that confident," Meghan replied.

"Which is what will make you a great Firemancer, Meghan."

"Um... how?"

"It shows me that you are not arrogant and will not abuse the power that comes with being a Firemancer."

Meghan's heart nearly stopped. She did not know how to respond. *Power?*

"Meghan, breathe, please," pleaded Juliska, upon seeing her face turn pale.

Meghan did so and looked into Juliska's eyes.

"I know a thousand equally frightening and confusing thoughts are rushing through your brain right now. Would you like some time…"

"No," exhaled Meghan. "I'm okay. Just, definitely caught me off guard. This was not what I expected in the least! Not that I expected anything specific, I just… "

"I realize that what I am about to ask of you, is again, too much, and certainly not simple. Moreover, I fully realize you have much yet to learn. We are living in desperate days, Meghan. Without my visions, I fear for the survival of my people. I need you to be my eyes, Meghan. I need you to see what I cannot. Our very existence may well rely upon it."

"That's not adding any pressure or anything," Meghan blurted without a second thought.

Juliska covered her mouth as if not to laugh.

Meghan could not help it and laughed, nervously.

"I'm sorry," Meghan tried to apologize, in between fits of laughter. "I guess it's a little overwhelming." She bit her lip, regaining control. "Do you really think I can do this?"

"Completely confident," Juliska stated. "You know, I was about your age when I began an apprenticeship with my own teacher. To be fair though, you are still new to this world, and I was told from birth what I was."

"You had a Firemancer as a teacher then, too?" asked Meghan.

"A seer, yes. A Firemancer, no. Firemancy is not as common as you, or I, make it seem. The ability is passed down from mothers only to their daughters."

"It's a family thing?" Meghan already knew this; however, it was Uncle Eddy, their ghostly and secret tutor in Grimble that had explained, so she pretended not to know. "So my mother was a Firemancer, too?"

"Do you know nothing of your mother at all?" prodded Juliska. "I have to admit I have been very curious."

Meghan replied honestly. "I don't really know anything... but, I am learning that even with my gift of sight, I seem to know less and less about everything."

"Well, I have to be honest, getting this secret off my chest is more of a relief than I could have imagined. My people have enough to worry about. If they discovered that their leader had lost her visions..." she did not finish.

"What do you need me to do?" Meghan asked. "Where do I start?"

"By moving in with me again, actually."

Meghan perked up. "I'll go pack my things," she replied, and then paused, remembering her brother. *Colin will be fine. He's busy guarding Catrina anyway.*

"We start first thing tomorrow," Juliska told her, bringing her back into the moment.

"So what's in there?" asked Meghan, nodding in the direction of the trunk with the ornate doorways.

Juliska smiled. "*That* will be one of our first lessons. I think you're going to like it," she hinted mischievously.

##

Meghan's nerves buzzed with anticipation as she departed Juliska's tent. Moments later, Nona appeared.

"Good hunting?" Meghan's thoughts asked her loyal Catawitch.

Nona licked her lips and grinned in reply. "You're going to pack, I presume," Nona asked Meghan. She had already heard the entire conversation through her connection with Meghan's thoughts.

"Yes, Nona. I wonder if Juliska realized you would still be able to hear my thoughts. She told me that everything we said to each other in her room was completely secret and could not be overheard."

"I am sure your conversations are safe from others, but the connection we have is not breakable, by any known magic," Nona informed Meghan. "But it does make me curious…"

"About what?"

"Whether Colin would be able to hear you as well?"

"Hm, I wonder. I haven't ever told Juliska about being able to read Colin's mind."

"And I think for now, that is one secret that should remain," Nona said.

"I agree," smiled Meghan. "Pretty crazy though, huh Nona?"

"Juliska's lack of visions concerns me greatly. Not only for what it means to everyone's safety, but also to yours."

"She is under a great deal of pressure, Nona. I mean, can you even imagine living day to day with the knowledge that it's *your* responsibility to protect all of these people?"

"And now, in part, it is also yours," Nona reminded.

"I will do whatever I can to help Juliska. I just feel so… not ready!"

"We will do this task, together. You know I will help you in whatever manner I can."

"Really don't know how I ever lived without you, Nona."

Nona rubbed up against her leg returning the compliment.

"How about we take it one step at a time," her Catawitch advised, sensing Meghan's nervousness rising again.

"Right," Meghan agreed. "First: pack. Second: move. Tomorrow..."

"One step at a time," Nona repeated kindly.

A short while later they arrived at the Mochrie tent.

"Hi, Mireya," Meghan said upon entering.

"Oh, hi," she replied, lifting her head from a book.

"Your parents gone?"

"At a zone meeting."

Meghan continued into their shared room, confused by the scene unfolding inside.

"What are you doing?" Meghan asked her brother.

"Packing, obviously," he replied.

"Yeah, figured that much out on my own. Why are you packing?"

"I decided to take up an offer from Billie, for me to stay with her for awhile. The Mochrie's tent is a little crowded, and she's got a free room." He leaned in. "It's better for Catrina. You could come with me if you want."

"Not like Colin took up any room in here, anyway," joked Jae. "Always sleeping outside. But, Billie's place is probably a little safer," he agreed.

"Well, there's no need for me to move into Billie's, as I have had another offer. I guess your tent is going to be a lot less crowded after today, Jae."

"Where are you ..." Colin did not finish, but rather sighed. "You're going to stay with Juliska again, aren't you?"

"Yes. She asked to me to do so, in order to continue my training as a Firemancer."

Meghan felt Colin nudging through her thoughts. She blocked him out, smirking.

"Where is Catrina?" she asked him in a whisper.

"Billie's. I left her there after Billie showed me the room and insisted I take it. She's taking a nap I think."

Meghan sensed his eagerness to return to her.

"We need to remember to thank your parents, Jae, for letting us stay with you. And who knows, we might be back," Meghan said.

"I'll pass the message along," he offered. "This will be strange, though. We've been living together for a long time. Can't say it won't be nice to have a little extra space though," he added, keeping the conversation lighthearted.

The three laughed.

"It has been quite the adventure," Meghan said, as if it were all coming to an end.

"You're acting like we're moving away permanently," Colin told her. "It's not like we're leaving. Just be a few tents over."

"Oh, I know," she said. "But in a way, we are sort of all going our separate ways. It's a little scary," she said honestly.

"Leave it to my dad to be right," Jae said begrudgingly.

Meghan and Colin waited for him to explain.

"Nothing stays the same forever, so don't get used to anything."

"That is actually a little depressing if you think about it," Meghan replied.

"And sadly, these days, very true!" Colin added.

"Well, you two have fun," Jae said, while falling backwards onto his sleeping cot. "I'll be kicking back and enjoying all this peace and quiet." He let out a fake bemoaning sigh. And yet there was a strange foreboding behind his words. Both Meghan and Colin felt it. Jae joked, but at the same time, they got the feeling that he seemed pleased about their departure. Something about the moment sent shivers down their spines.

"Was that your bad feeling or mine?" Colin asked his sister through their thoughts.

"Let's not go there again!" she shot back. "I don't need any more bad omens."

Meghan blocked her mind, losing all confidence. *What am I doing? Leaving Colin to fend for himself. Taking on a life I'm not ready for. What happened to getting back home? Figuring out what happened to Uncle Arnon?*

Nona touched her hand, jostling Meghan back into reality. Nona jumped down from the cot and Meghan grabbed her bag. She opened up her thoughts to Colin. "Be careful," she sent him.

"You, too."

"We might not be staying in the same place, but whenever you need me... I'll hear you, I promise!" she told him.

Colin nodded. He gently patted Jae's shoulder, and rushed out of the tent, yelling a quick "see you later" to Mireya.

Minutes later, Meghan did the same. Jae followed her out and waved goodbye, alongside his sister.

Mireya sighed, leaning her head on his shoulder.

"It is kind of sad, isn't it?" he whispered.

"Yes. But it's not just them leaving."

Jae put his arm around his sister.

"I know. But maybe once we find out what's happened here, some things will get back to normal."

"Like play time," she giggled.

"Yes! Definitely that," he agreed heartily.

"I just hate sitting around, waiting and waiting. I wish there were some way I could help. *To do something!*" Mireya said.

"I know what you mean," he replied. "But we have to let the Initiated take care of this. The best thing we can do is keep our eyes and ears at the ready, and study hard. So when the time comes, we can do our part."

Mireya picked up her book and bonked Jae on the head with it.

"I have read this book so many times I practically have it memorized," she said.

"Ah, key word – practically!"

She shot him an ugly face, stuck out her tongue and started reading again.

Jae let her read in silence, staring at the tent wall while deep in thought.

His sister had it right. He wanted to do his part, too. He wanted to help. He wanted enough power to make a difference. *Perhaps I should take the Banon up on her offer... She did say I was perfect for the job.* Jae shook his head in confused indecision. *She also said it would be dangerous...*

Jae's heart raced. *We face danger every day! Besides, once Dad knows I accepted a job from the Banon, he'll have to be satisfied.*

"I'll be back in a little while," Jae said suddenly, arising from his chair. He did not give Mireya a chance to question him. He darted through the meadow searching for the tent he needed. He froze just outside the entrance, unsure whether to knock or just enter. A withered hand pulled back the canvas door and a whiff of mothballs struck Jae's nostrils.

"Please enter, young Jae Mochrie," said a voice, from inside. "But only if you are certain. For as you have been warned, this choice is final and cannot be undone."

Jae's heart pounded. All he had to do was step inside. His thoughts took him back to his conversation with the Banon months previous.

"I have seen your true heart, Jae, and I understand, more than most, what it is you desire."

"But, it feels wrong," he admitted sheepishly. "Like something I should be able to control."

"Maybe you are not meant to control it," the Banon posed. "Perhaps your experience of being left behind and fending for yourself was meant to happen, to change the course of your life for the better."

Jae had never thought about it that way before.

The Banon continued. "I see it as passion, Jae. And if people did not have passion for power, how would the world ever find its leaders? Power rises to the top, yes. And there's no argument that many in power are consumed by it. But power is not purely good or purely bad."

Jae was glad he had finally dared have this conversation.

"I guess that's true," he said. "I mean, look at you," he said with reverence. "*You* are what we are all supposed to be striving to be like. I guess that can't be bad."

Juliska just smiled her reply, pleased.

"I just know I could do so much, if only given the chance," he told her.

"I can make that happen," she replied.

Now, the choice was up to Jae.

He could study, graduate, and wait for his Initiation, or he could step through this door and bypass years of waiting for his life to begin. Jae knew no more, other than once he stepped through, the decision was final and that he would face unimaginable dangers. But it also meant skipping ahead and never looking back.

"Well... I don't have all day," the voice echoed out of the tent impatiently. "What's it going to be?"

Jae grinned and then stepped inside, letting the canvas door close behind him.

Chapter Three

Colin arrived at Billie's tent. She greeted him at the door.

"Hi, Billie. Back with my stuff." It was not much, just a backpack and a small trunk.

"Sure am glad ya said yes," she told him.

"It was getting a bit crowded at the Mochrie's," Colin replied.

"You make yourself right at home, now. I have a meetin' to get off to, but I'll be home 'round evening." She winked and left Colin to get settled.

Catrina slept through the afternoon. It was the first uninterrupted sleep she had been able to have since Colin had saved her from the cave.

Evening came and Billie did not come home.

Catrina woke briefly and Colin told her he would grab them some dinner. When he returned she was sitting up in bed, but still looked tired.

Catrina yawned.

"You should get more rest," insisted Colin.

She did not argue. "I've never felt so tired," she muttered, sinking into her blanket.

Colin grabbed another blanket, taking a seat on the ground next to the bed, but sleep evaded him. Instead, he stared dreamily at Catrina while she slept, soundly.

What would happen once people discovered her? It was bound to happen.

He feared that moment.

Would he be able to protect her?

Did she know why she had been put into the glass coffin?

He hoped that after Catrina felt rested and recovered, he would finally get some answers. He leaned his head, resting it on the side of the bed, and at some point, while watching Catrina, his eyes closed and sleep came over him.

Meghan awoke the next morning to the sounds of a heated discussion just outside her room. Her sleep had been spotty, at best. A terrible feeling had been nagging at the back of her mind all night regarding her brother.

Before she could even speak, Nona jumped onto the bed.

"I already took care of it!" the Catawitch said in reply, to the task Meghan had not even officially asked her to do yet.

"Still don't know what I'd do without you, Nona."

"Nor I, you," she returned. "Your dreams were vivid and I agreed with your thinking. Therefore, I checked on Colin this morning and all is well. I will keep an eye on him just the same. Trust your senses, Meghan. I do."

"I just feel like something horrible is about to happen to him, Nona. But I can't sit around worrying about him every minute, when I have so much to learn."

"Which is why you will leave this task to me."

Meghan touched her forehead to Nona's, saying thanks.

While dressing, she turned her attention back to the debate going on in the tent's front room.

"Our food supply is running dangerously low," a man's voice spoke. "And, I'm sure you all noticed the lack of stores nearby. Growing food is our only option. Although, without knowing what's going on, or how long we will be here, growing may not be a viable option." Meghan recognized this voice as Darius Hadrian, from the Viancourt.

"It would be viable if you would allow me to use magic," a female retorted. "The food could be ready in weeks rather than months!"

"We have already been over this! We have tested it before. Food grown by magic, lacking the normal growing period, also lacks proper taste and nutrition. It's not real food!" the first man argued.

"Would you rather have NO food?" the woman spat.

Darius sighed, giving in. "No, of course not. We cannot go hungry. Banon Blackwell, I will leave this choice up to you. Sadly, I fear we may have no choice, as it may come down to a choice of low-quality food versus no food."

"Even if we do decide to use magic," spoke a man's voice, "there is still the matter of gathering enough magical energy to do so. We still have to address the issue of our weakening magic. Our emergency stores are also at dangerously low levels."

The room went silent. Meghan took a quick peek out of her door. The group sat at the long wooden table, facing the Banon, waiting for her to reply.

"Whatever is decided here today, we must all remain calm," she insisted. "We have already prohibited the use of magic for the investigation. For now, this will keep the people fairly in the dark as to how weakened we are. There is no need to cause extra alarm."

She paused, pondering for just a moment.

"Grow the garden, but be sure not to use more than half the magical stores we have left. We simply must not leave ourselves without some form of defense… especially if our magic continues to weaken."

Everyone nodded in agreement.

"Meanwhile, I shall form a hunting party," she continued. "We can spare a few Balaton, and perhaps they can find us some food in the forest."

The meeting came to a hasty close and everyone departed, leaving Juliska alone. Meghan waited for a few minutes before leaving her room, not wanting to cast suspicions that she had been listening. When she came out, Juliska squelched her concerns.

"Good morning, Meghan. Sorry. I am afraid you will hear many heated conversations in the coming days. Please, do not worry yourself about it though. Just all in a days work."

"Sounds pretty serious, though."

"Serious, yes. Something we have not experienced before, no. We will persevere. We always do." She sounded weary in her reply. "While we are being serious, there's something I wanted to tell you. Sit, please."

Meghan sat down across from her.

"I feel that I have put a tremendous pressure on you, and for this I apologize."

Meghan opened her mouth to speak but Juliska motioned for her to wait.

"I just wanted to impress upon you how grateful I am that you are willing to help us. To help me. Just a little over a year ago, you did not even know magic existed, and now here you are stuck in the middle of this mess. I also need you to know, that I... that I do not just think of you as a Firemancer, someone that can help me do my job. You are a bright, talented young woman, no doubt."

She paused, as if searching for the right words to continue.

"Sorry, I don't know why, but this is hard for me to admit. My reputation is not that of the motherly type. I am tough, blunt and do not apologize for it. As I have said before, I must be if we are to survive. However, I want you to feel as though you can be open with me. Honest. To all ends good or bad. I want to be there for you as a person, not just as your teacher."

"O-Okay," Meghan stammered, barely able to choke out her reply. Then, more boldly, she added, "To be honest, I think motherly is exactly what you are. Tough and blunt, sure. You just have a lot more children to watch over than most mothers do."

Juliska looked perplexed. "I have never really thought of it like that, Meghan. You are really quite wise."

"I guess being a big sister comes with its perks," she muttered, shrugging.

"Just as long as you know that I am here for you. Whatever you need." Juliska took hold of Meghan's hand, lovingly. She then let go and took a deep breath. "I am afraid I must delay our training for a short while, as I must depart. While I am away there is something I would like you to read, in your pocket guide."

Meghan hastened into her room and came back to the table with the Firemancer's Pocket Guide in hand. Juliska grabbed it and flipped through the pages.

"Here we are," she said, handing the book back to Meghan.

"*Calling*," Meghan read aloud.

"Study that chapter thoroughly," Juiliska ordered. "Tomorrow, we will revisit the trunk in my room and discuss it further. An eager gleam in Juliska's eye caught Meghan's attention, and she wished greatly they could go right then.

Meghan sighed, feeling guilty. *Is it wrong to feel this happy, with so many terrible things going on? People are missing. I have the most important task of my life ahead of me. Colin is hiding a girl that someone tried to leave behind in a cave rarely visited by humans.*

The rush of emotion suddenly overwhelmed her and tears streamed down her face. She was thankful, at least, for being alone and crept into her room. After gushing non-stop for nearly an hour, she dried her eyes and drank a glass of water.

Meghan opened her book and began reading the chapter on *calling*.

After awhile her stomach growled, so she left the tent to grab a bite to eat. She hoped to run into Colin but did not see him. Nona did find her though, and followed her home. They curled up on Meghan's bed and Nona fell asleep as Meghan set in again to reading. Hours passed and day turned into evening.

"Meetings sure do last a long time around here," Meghan whispered. "I wonder if I should wait up?"

"I imagine Juliska would want you to rest," Nona told her. "Especially if there are to be many repeats of this mornings early meeting."

"You're probably right. Besides, I really want to know what's in that trunk. Right now tomorrow seems ages away!"

"Why don't you read just a little more while I go check on your brother? Maybe I'll be lucky and scurry up a juicy rodent along the way."

"Have fun," Meghan said, putting her nose back into her book. As the evening air set into the meadow, a chill came over her. Almost as if requested, Pantin Hollee arrived with some papers to leave for the Banon, and offered to start the stove for Meghan. Within minutes, she had the tent perfectly toasty.

"Just add a big log in about ten minutes, it'll keep going well into the night," she told Meghan.

"Thanks! You are multi-talented, Hollee."

"Part of the job," she winked and then departed as quickly as she had appeared. Meghan waited the ten minutes and threw the log into the stove. The heat felt so good that it never even occurred to her to be careful around the flames.

Her next memory was that of someone shaking her.

Meghan lay curled up on the cold ground. She had fallen into a vision and slept through the entire night. Her hand rested against the now cool stove. The fire had died sometime during the night.

"Ah. Great! You!" she muttered, gathering herself.

"Yes, it seems I have picked you up off the ground, once again." Ivan Crane eyed her sternly.

"Should have known *you* would find me, seeing as I'm having *your* nightmare again!" She spoke more harshly than she'd meant to.

However, frustrations brought on by Ivan keeping secrets about Jae Mochrie were not what she needed right now. "So is there a purpose to your *timely* visit?"

"Report for the Banon. She asked me to meet her. I'm a few minutes early."

"Awesome," muttered Meghan.

"You're in an even worse mood than normal," noted Ivan.

"And you know why!"

The conversation ended as footsteps approached.

"Banon Blackwell," Ivan spoke, bowing his head slightly upon her entrance.

"Perfect! Ivan. Follow me, please. Meghan, don't stray far. I will not be long and we must get started right away this morning." She disappeared into her room, followed by Ivan Crane.

While Meghan waited, it dawned on her that Juliska must not have returned home the night before, and wondered what could have kept her busy all night.

Minutes later, Ivan exited her room.

"She wants to see you now," he told Meghan dryly. She did not wait for him to leave and swiped by him and into Juliska's room.

"Let's get right down to business, shall we?" Juliska said, opening the trunk with the two doors. She unlocked the door on the left and stepped inside.

Meghan tentatively followed. It took a moment for her eyes to adjust, as wherever they were, it was dark. Then, it started to lighten, one candle flame at a time.

As the flames flickered and her eyes adjusted, Meghan realized she was standing in a stone cave. There were hundreds of thin pillars, and at the top of each pillar was a candle. Each candle took the shape of people, things or places.

"Welcome to a Firemancer's lair," began Juliska. "One day, you will have one of your own."

Meghan stared in stunned disbelief. She stepped closer to one of the candles, which took the shape of a meadow. As she peered into the orange flame, the colors began to shift, turning gold and then black. What stunned her most was the picture that appeared in the flames: people, bustling through a familiar looking meadow.

"Is this the meadow we are camped in, right now? Is this what's going on, outside in the meadow?"

"Yes. It is," was Juliska's simple reply.

Meghan walked through the room, peering into flame after flame. After awhile, Juliska continued.

"Normally, you would not be shown this until much later in your training. However, the circumstances we find ourselves in force my hand. Moreover, I think you're ready. This here," she waved her hand around her head, "is a Firemancer's most prized possession. Our arsenal if you wish."

Meghan listened intently.

"Not that the visions we have are any less vital. But these flames allow us to see more than just the future."

"It feels like spying," Meghan admitted self-consciously.

"Only if you spy," replied Juliska.

"Huh?"

"It's understandable to be confused by this. You must learn, though, that there is a difference between spying and watching over someone. Making the meadow candle was a difficult choice for me. But seeing as my visions are not working, I felt it necessary to use the tools at my disposal to keep a closer eye on things."

Meghan tried to understand but still felt as though she was spying on her neighbors.

"The key, Meghan, as with any power we are handed, is how we choose to use that power. As a leader, I must make choices that from the outside do not always appear fair. In time, you'll come to understand what I mean."

"What you say makes sense, I just ..."

"Feel creepy? Nosy? Intrusive?" Juliska asked knowingly.

"Yeah, that about says it," Meghan sighed. "I think I do understand though," she added. She did feel she understood, but still didn't feel comfortable spying on people. Her thoughts instantly strayed to Colin and Catrina. How could Juliska not have noticed something odd?

"So what are these other candles?" she asked, moving forward.

"My greatest assets, Meghan. Fire is our most valuable tool, weapon and mode of communication. I assume you read the chapter on *calling?*"

"Repeatedly," Meghan answered.

Juliska motioned Meghan to approach a candle.

"Is that... is that Pantin Hollee?"

"Yes. When I need my Pantin, I simply go to her flame and *call* for her. This can be tricky, as most people are unaware of the Firemancer's *call*. They hear it as more of a distant echo or thought, like a dream. Hollee, however, is aware of *calling*, and expects it at any time, day or night."

"Can you call her now? So I can see?" Juliska smiled and let her gaze fall into the flame above the Pantin's candle.

"Hollee," she spoke, just as if she were standing in the same room.

Hollee's head did not move, but she did call out. "Yes, Banon Blackwell."

"How close are we to being ready with those announcements?"

"Within the hour," she replied, still working.

"Thank you, Hollee. I'll let you get back to work."

Juliska turned to Meghan.

"There. See."

"That is amazing!" Meghan said. "How long did it take you to master Calling?"

"To be honest, it took awhile. Some parts were very easy for me, others took many months of practice. And it goes so much farther than what I have just shown you."

Meghan now began to see the benefits of the room, beyond the initial fear of spying. Many sudden thoughts clouded her mind at this moment, however. Did Juliska have a candle of her, or Colin? Could she master this power and *call* home? Could she speak to Sebastien? Or Kanda Macawi? Could she find out their Uncle Arnon's fate?

She also realized that while in Limbo, she had unknowingly *called* Sebastien. She had actually made contact with him. That really did happen. *I need to master this as soon as possible! Maybe I can't go home, but maybe I can call home!*

The look on Meghan's face caused Juliska to chuckle.

"If I had a picture of my own face, when I was first shown the possibilities of my power, you would notice an extreme likeness to the look on your face right now."

"Sorry, it's just... overwhelming. I don't really know where to start."

"We start at the beginning," Juliska said. "Practice. Study. And more practice." Juliska handed her a candle.

"I made this for you yesterday. This will get you started."

"It's me!" cried Meghan.

"Yes. It is how I learned and how you will learn, without the fear of unnecessary spying. All you will see, if successful, is yourself."

Meghan did feel relieved, but at the same time, worried. This meant Juliska might well have other candles of her, or Colin. He needed to be extra careful.

"One day," said Juliska, "I will teach you how to create the candles, but for now, I want you to practice diligently with this single candle. If you have questions, write them down. We will discuss them in our next session."

"Okay," Meghan replied, dreamily staring at the candle.

"I am afraid that once again, duty calls and our training will have to continue another time. I can hear Pantin Hollee *calling* me."

"She can do that, too? It works both ways?" Meghan asked in awe.

Juliska laughed lightly.

"Welcome to a larger world, Meghan... Welcome to the life of a Firemancer."

##

Colin and Catrina awoke to the sounds of Billie Sadorus rummaging through belongings. Colin could not make out what she was saying, but could hear panic in her voice.

"I'll go see what's up," he said. Outside his room, he noticed drag marks leading into the tent. Billie sat over an open trunk, crazily pulling out item after item.

"Not her. Oh please not her," she repeatedly whispered.

"Can I help you find something, Billie?"

The normally controlled Billie jumped, apparently forgetting that Colin was there. Her face gave away her fear, but she quickly got to her feet.

"Everything's fine," she told him. "Nothing to fret about!"

"Um. Okay." He noticed that she clutched a picture frame to her chest as she spoke. She gently dropped the frame into the trunk and disappeared into her room. Colin took a glance at the picture.

Catrina stepped up beside him.

"I know this picture," he told her quietly.

"You know who this is?"

"Well, no, not who. But this is the same woman, in another picture, that I saw at Billie's a while back."

"She must mean a lot to Billie then." Catrina noticed the drag marks. "Colin, where did this trunk come from?"

"I think it came from the meadow. I think…"

"That it belonged to the woman in the picture…" Catrina finished with a sigh.

"Poor Billie. Poor everyone," Colin whispered. "Chances are everyone in this caravan knows someone from the missing group."

"Yes, it is quite sad," Catrina agreed.

Just then, footsteps ran by the tent, just outside.

A voice called out. "Meeting! Meeting! Right now! Everyone must attend!"

More footsteps followed as everyone eagerly hurried to attend. Billie came out of her room, seeming back to her normal self again, and they followed her. Everyone gathered in the cantina in the center of the meadow.

Colin avoided the crowd, and stayed at the edge of the group, with Catrina at his side.

Whispers raced through the crowd.

"I heard that the hunting party never returned!"

"Really?"

"When did they leave?"

"Last night I think," someone said back.

"What hunting party?" a man asked.

"Do you ever know what's going on?" his wife replied in a snarky tone.

"Maybe they've found out some other news," another voice muttered.

Jae sidled up next to Colin. "My guess is the hunting party," he whispered. "They left yesterday and were supposed to be back by dark. There's been no sign of them. At least that's what I heard my dad tell my mom this morning."

"That can't be good," Colin muttered back.

Jae shuffled his hand through his hair, pulling it away from his face. Catrina nudged Colin's arm and pointed to Jae's face.

"What happened, Jae?" asked Colin, seeing a bruise on his chin.

"Huh?"

"Your face, there's a huge bruise on your chin."

"Oh, that. Fell, chin first, into the corner of my cot."

"Bummer," Colin said.

"That bruise is not from hitting his cot," Catrina said. "It's much too large."

Colin shrugged, unable to answer her without someone overhearing.

"You know what, I forgot something I gotta take care of," Jae suddenly said. He took off and was out of sight in seconds.

"I thought this was a mandatory meeting?" Catrina whispered.

"Yeah, me too," Colin muttered under his breath. "Jae knows what he's doing I guess." They turned their attention back to the meeting, as Pantin Hollee jumped up onto a table, so everyone could see her as she spoke.

Colin noted Kalila and Kalida Jackal near the front, ready to take notes for their next addition of the Jackal Lantern.

The crowd instantly silenced, waiting for the Pantin to begin.

"I speak today, for Banon Juliska Nandalia Blackwell," she said first. "You may have heard that we sent out a hunting party, in search of food. I can confirm that as of this time, they have not yet returned."

Worried murmurs spread like wildfire.

"Though we are of course concerned, we do not yet believe anything unfortunate has occurred. They could simply be lost."

A few people agreed with this reasoning, but most clearly believed something sinister had occurred.

"The most likely scenario is that they are delayed. However, as a precaution, the Viancourt has seen fit to enforce the following rules, effective immediately!"

She paused while unrolling a scroll and began reading.

"One: Absolutely no one is permitted to leave the meadow. Two: Magic will continue to be prohibited, so the investigation into the whereabouts of our sister caravan can continue, unimpeded. Three: Each and every member of this caravan will be expected to report, directly to the Viancourt, *any suspicious activity!*"

Hollee rolled up the scroll. "The curfew is lifted, for now," she added, "but we impress upon each and every one of you to be cautious when out after dark. That is all."

"What do you mean by suspicious activity?" Kalila Jackal called out. "Is it believed that someone here is responsible for the devastation in the meadow?"

"No. No. Of course not," Hollee replied compassionately. "But to be blunt, we need all eyes and ears open! We are each equally responsible for our own actions as well as reporting the actions of others, that could potentially be dangerous to the group as a whole."

"Beautifully spoken," Kalida replied. "I'm going to quote that."

The Pantin nodded her approval.

"Now disperse. Zone leaders, gather your members. Meetings will resume in an hour's time. Be safe! Be cautious! Be alert! That is all for now."

The Pantin hopped down from the table and continued on her way to fulfilling her next duty.

Colin let go of Catrina's hand, attempting to look like he walked alone, as the crowd dispersed across the meadow. Each conversation he overheard was about either the missing hunting party or the missing caravan. He nodded hello as he passed by the Jackal sisters, scribbling notes, for what was sure to be an extra special edition of the Jackal Lantern.

While walking back toward Billie's, they stumbled into a group of youngsters. Darcy led the conversation.

"I can't believe we still can't use magic! What the heck are we supposed to do all day?"

"I know, right," Dulcy agreed. "I mean, if I have to style my own hair one more day, I am going to freak out!"

"Dulcy," Darcy spoke dryly. "Shut up. Listening to you speak is starting to irritate me."

The youngsters laughed, but suppressed it after the look Darcy threw at them.

"It is a pain," another boy added. "I'm sick of spending all my time cleaning up the meadow, and by hand."

"And not playing any games," another girl chimed in.

"Yeah, I'm bored out of my mind!" a boy next to her agreed.

Colin debated taking the long way back to Billie's, to avoid the group, or mainly, avoid Darcy, but stopped when Jae emerged from around the corner. To Colin's and the group's surprise, Jae confronted them.

"You're really going to complain about not using magic?" Jae asked in a composed manner.

Something about the expression on Jae's face frightened Colin.

Darcy spun around and confronted Jae. "And what are *you* going to do about it?"

Jae did not reply. He just stared into Darcy's eyes.

After a second, her eyes narrowed, filling first with fear, turning into confusion and then, denial. She blew it off, grabbing Dulcy.

"Whatever, weirdo!"

Colin noticed that she turned her head, just enough to glance at Jae with growing curiosity as she walked away. "There's something seriously wrong with that guy," she whispered as she and Dulcy passed by Colin. "What are you looking at?" she barked at him.

He replied by smiling back at her, as if to say *have a nice day*, which of course, just infuriated her even more. Rather than retorting, she just huffed and stormed away.

"As for the rest of you," Jae continued, "isn't there something more important you could all be doing?"

Colin was not the only one to notice the change in Jae's attitude, but no one questioned him. The group went their separate ways. Jae walked straight past Colin, as if he were suddenly as invisible as Catrina.

"I can't believe I'm saying this," Colin couldn't help but admit, "but I have to agree with Darcy on this one. Something about Jae isn't right."

"How long has this behavior been going on?" Catrina asked.

"I forget you haven't known everyone that long," Colin said. "It's hard to say, really. I mean, my sister has had terrible visions about Jae, but she has never really gone into depth about them. Only that she's very worried."

"Maybe its nothing," Catrina suggested. "Perhaps he is just trying to do his part... you know, spying on his neighbors and all," she said mockingly.

Colin rolled his eyes.

"That's not going to make our lives any simpler, is it? Still, I should try to get Meghan a message. Let her know what happened, just in case."

##

Seconds after stepping into Billie's tent, Nona bounded in behind them.

"Colin, I have a message from your sister," her cattish voice spoke.

"Oddly enough, I have one for her as well," Colin replied, glad of the Catawitch's timely visit. "How is she doing, Nona?" he asked first.

"She is fine. However, she tried to reach your thoughts, but was unable."

"Oh, how strange. I didn't even feel her try," he said truthfully.

"Actually, this proves a theory," Nona explained. "There is a room in which Meghan does her training, and while she's in there, no one can hear or see what happens. *We* can still hear each other's thoughts while she is in this room. However, it appears that whatever magic protects this room, blocks your telepathy."

"But you guys can still hear each other?" Colin confirmed. "Nothing has ever blocked our telepathy before, except for us."

"Yes. It is a disconcerting situation on my part, as I feel more confident knowing that Meghan can always reach you, if needed."

"Yeah, I agree. After Grimble... well, I just don't want to go through something like that again."

"Which brings me to the real reason for my visit." Her voice quieted, as she stalked about the room, listening for anyone close by.

"Is it safe?" Colin asked her.

"Yes. There is no one close enough to hear."

Colin decided to undo Catrina's invisibility spell and she materialized in front of Nona.

"Hello, Catrina. It is nice to *see* you," Nona's cat-like voice said playfully.

"Honestly, it is nice to be seen, Nona, and it's lovely to see you as well. So what brings you here?"

"I come bearing a warning," she shared.

"A warning?" Colin repeated, dismayed.

"Yes. It is possible that you are being watched."

"It seems like everyone is being watched," Catrina said. "Now more than ever, especially after this mornings meeting."

"Yes, definitely more so. But this is different, Colin."

"How so?"

"Meghan has discovered that there are ways, which we did not previously know about, to spy on someone. To watch their every move if desired."

"Let me guess? Juliska has something to do with this?" asked Catrina, folding her arms in disdain.

Without hesitation, Colin recast the spell, once again hiding Catrina.

"Do they know about her?" he asked, his nostrils flaring.

"We have no reason to believe they do. Meghan does not know with any certainty that you are actually being watched. She just wanted you to be aware that it is possible."

Colin started pacing.

"It will be okay, Colin," Catrina said, trying to comfort him. Her eyes gave away the fear she truly felt.

"I just do not understand what my sister sees in Juliska Blackwell!" he shouted too loudly. "I have said it before and I'll say it again: I do not trust her! Not one bit!"

"Colin," Nona began. "It's not always so simple."

"Well it should be!"

Colin calmed himself.

"I'm sorry, Nona. I didn't mean to get angry. I just don't know what to do."

Catrina grasped his hand. "We'll figure it out together, Colin. Your sister loves you. This is why she sent Nona. You know she would never do anything to put you in danger."

"I do understand Colin," Nona said, not having heard Catrina. "Just be careful. I must return now. You said you had a message for Meghan."

Colin explained Jae's odd behavior.

"I will pass this information along, Colin. I can tell you though, that Meghan knows nothing more. It is a situation she finds most infuriating."

"Thanks, Nona. Take care, okay?"

"You as well," she replied, jaunting out of the tent.

As soon as they were alone Colin grabbed Catrina and darted into their room. He used every magical spell he could find in the Magicante to protect the room from outsiders.

"I didn't want to say this in front of Nona," Colin finally admitted, "but I really think my sister's relationship with Juliska Blackwell is not healthy."

"Like it or not though, Juliska is the only other seer around. Meghan does need a teacher."

"You're right, I know. There is just something that I can't quite put my finger on, Catrina. Something about Juliska that's just… off." It was not the right word, but his anger kept him from thinking straight.

"And if Meghan is right?" Catrina whispered. "What then?"

"We could leave?"

"We don't have anywhere to go, Colin."

"There must be a way," he said, stomping his foot.

"We would somehow have to get our hands on the Book of Doorways," Catrina said. "It's the only way I know of to find a way out of this place."

"We'll never get our hands on that book!" Colin's voice trembled. "It's in Juliska's possession. She's the only one that uses it to open the doorways."

"Then we must be very careful, Colin. I cannot be discovered, not yet."

She tried to hide her fear, but as she spoke, Colin could tell she was afraid.

Colin stepped toward Catrina, to comfort her, when the ground began to tremble under their feet. The tremble worsened into shaking, which spread out of the tent and across the meadow.

Alarmed screams nearly drowned out the rumble accompanying the quake. Colin steadied himself, ran to the outer room and stuck his head out of the tent, only to pull it back in when a nearby tent pole came crashing down in front of him. He turned around to find Catrina standing right behind him. She took hold of him and he drew her in, holding her close. She closed her eyes, as if to wish away the quake. Colin felt his own panic start to lessen.

The ground slowly began to stabilize again.

The rumble dissipated.

Outside of the tent, they heard voices calling out, asking if everyone was okay, and people scurrying to check on loved ones. Colin stuck his head out of the tent again, and it seemed that everyone was uninjured. A few things had fallen over, but overall, everything was okay.

He felt Meghan reaching into his thoughts and opened up the block.

"Are you guys okay?" she asked.

"Yes!" he replied quickly. "And you?"

"Fine. Was that freaky or what? We've never experienced a quake before."

"Not in a hurry to have it happen again," Colin replied. "Since you're in my head though, thanks for the warning."

"Nona thinks I pretty much scared you to death. Sorry. I just meant for you to be extra careful. They are watching *everyone* right now, Colin! It's like everything is falling to pieces."

"Yeah, that's kind of what it feels like here, too," he admitted. Hearing Meghan's voice calmed him. He was wrong to get so upset. Somehow, things would work out.

"I gotta run, Col. Just glad you're all right."

"You too, Sis."

He felt her mind go blank and put his own block back in place. Colin explained to Catrina that his sister's warning might have come across a bit heavier than she had meant it to.

"Maybe I should go see if anyone needs help," he said, feeling the need to keep busy.

"Yes, go. I will be okay here."

Colin looked pained at leaving her.

"Really, Colin. I am fine. We are fine. We will just be careful. If I have to, I'll stay in this room until its safe to leave."

Colin nodded in begrudging acceptance. However, when he opened the tent to leave, he jumped back, startled.

"Ivan!"

"Sorry, didn't mean to frighten you," Ivan replied, stepping inside.

"I was just coming out to see if anyone needed help. Does this sort of thing happen here a lot?"

"Never been here before, don't know much about the place," Ivan replied. "But everyone is fine. A few broken things, tents that need reinforcing, but nothing serious. You both fared well I presume?"

"Yes. We're fine," Colin said.

"But that's not why Ivan's here," Catrina spoke, from behind Colin.

"Is she here?" Ivan asked, confirming Catrina's suspicions.

"Colin, could you lift the spell so Ivan can see and hear me, please. I assumed he would want to speak with me at some point."

"Let's go into our room first, just as a precaution," he advised.

Colin motioned for Ivan to follow.

Once inside Colin lifted the spell and Catrina materialized.

"I have some questions," he started right in.

"Of course," Catrina said.

The first question, however, was not what Colin expected. He had assumed Ivan wanted to know more about his mother.

"How did you end up in the cave?"

Colin listened intently, as they had not yet discussed this very intriguing issue.

"To be perfectly honest, Ivan, I am not totally sure. All I remember is taking a walk and then the next thing I knew, I'm waking up in a strange room. A hospital room, I think. I was surrounded by faces I did not know," she stopped, and clarified her last statement. "That's not completely accurate. I did recognize one face, but only from pictures. You are not going to like it, Ivan."

"I assume you're going to say Banon Blackwell," he said.

Catrina nodded yes.

"She is the only person I assumed you would have photographs of," he added.

"I know you probably want to know why, but I do not know, Ivan." Her voice echoed confidence. "All I am sure about is that I was given a drink which made me sleepy, and then I was put into the coffin. After that, everything is a bit foggy. All my memories are from dreams. Dreams that somehow found Colin Jacoby, while he slept in his own coma."

Colin could hear Ivan's teeth grinding as he contemplated what Catrina told him. Listening to her talk was both satisfying and terrifying for Colin. On the one hand, these were questions that he had desperately wanted to ask himself, but had not yet dared, for fear it would upset her. Somehow though, he also had the nagging suspicion that Catrina did not speak the entire truth. That she held something back from Ivan. Perhaps, when she was ready, she would tell him.

"And what about my mother?" Ivan blurted out. "How is it that she would leave this message with you, so many years ago, as an infant, to deliver it to me now? So many years past her death. And why you?"

"These are things I really cannot answer, Ivan. I wish I could. I really do. But, now that we have the time, I *can* tell you the entire message."

"Please," he begged. "Tell me."

"I am sure you recall the first part, 'Find my hidden treasure and you will find the answers you seek,'" she started. "This is the rest: 'To find my hidden treasure, you must seek the possession I held close to my heart.'"

"Another riddle! Why can't people just say what they mean?" he nearly shouted.

"I am truly sorry, Ivan. This is obviously something important, and I wish I knew more."

He eyed her as if she was holding back some vital part, something that would explain his late mother's message.

"I do not know what possession she speaks of," he sighed. "Many of the people who knew her are either dead or in another caravan. Are you sure there is nothing more?" he demanded.

"Ivan, I'm sure she told what she knows," Colin spoke coarsely.

"Yes, that is all Ivan," Catrina affirmed, again. She gently touched his arm. "Perhaps now is not the time for you to discover the answer," Catrina added, speaking wisely.

"You're a strange girl, Catrina Flummer," Ivan replied, in a calmer voice. "I will keep silent about your presence here, but I feel it only wise to warn you," he turned to Colin, "that with everything going on, keeping this secret will get harder each day that it continues."

"We don't need any more reminders about that," Colin exclaimed.

Ivan took his leave, once again leaving Colin and Catrina alone. Colin's first act was to redo the spell to hide her. He then took out the Magicante.

"What are you doing?" Catrina asked him.

"Heeding the warnings and getting us all the protection we need," he assured her.

She came and sat next to him and watched him open the book.

"Please, can you help me?" he asked. "I need to protect this tent, especially this room. I want it to be as if we don't exist to the outside world while we are in this room."

"Hmm," its cranky, tired voice replied. "It does appear that drastic measures are required in this matter." The books pages began to flip back and forth. Magicante did this repeatedly, offering various spells to help conceal the space and keep it safe. After thirty minutes, the Magicante flipped shut.

"There," Colin said, relieved. "It is as secure as we can make it!" Feeling bold, he questioned Catrina. "So... can I assume you did not actually tell Ivan everything?"

"You are right," she sighed. "Everything that was pertinent to Ivan, he now knows. As for the rest, I think it needs to remain secret. At least until I know, for sure, what exactly did happen to me and why. Even with my suspicions, I do not want to pass judgment before it is due. Is that okay?" she asked timidly.

"You know, I have to agree with Ivan," Colin said. "You really are a strange girl. No, not strange... unique ... in a very good way," he added, hoping he had not offended her.

"I just don't want to make things worse than they already are," she said. "I don't actually *want* to be strange," she smiled, taking his hand.

"I don't mind, really," he said. "I mean, being strange or not telling me everything," he clarified. He desired greatly to lean forward and kiss her, but kept his distance, his nerves getting the better of him.

Catrina however, did not have this same fear. She leaned in and gently kissed his lips just for a moment, and then rested her head on his shoulder.

"Your heart is beating quite fast," she whispered.

"Is it?" he stuttered.

Colin said nothing more, wishing he could stay in this moment forever.

Chapter Four

Sebastien Jendaya stood at the entrance of a cave.

"I can't believe I'm doing this," he muttered, looking as deeply as possible into the darkness that awaited him. "I can't believe this place is real."

The dream had seemed real though... real enough that he knew the moment he awoke that he had to find this place.

A voice echoed in his head.

"Please. Enter, Sebastien. I have been waiting for your arrival."

He stepped confidently into the darkness. After a short distance, he came to a dimly lit room. Sun shone down from a source above, but it only lit the center of the room. A dark-haired woman stood with her back to Sebastien, removing a whistling kettle of water from a stove.

Even in the dimly lit space, he could see that her hair was a deep black with hints of red.

"Tea?" she asked.

"No. Thanks."

"Take a seat then," she said, nodding her head toward a wooden table off to the side. He sat, breathlessly, waiting for her to join him. As she turned to face him, he gasped. *She looks just like* ... he did not dare finish the thought. *Her eyes.* He shook off his thoughts, as there could be no truth to them. Her eyes were bright blue, like a sparkling ocean, and even in the dim light of the cave, they were piercing against her pale skin and dark hair.

Sebastien did not wait for her to speak. "Why have you brought me here? Who are you?"

The woman took a moment to answer.

"I suppose the truth will have to suffice here, won't it? Although I have not spoken the truth in such a long time, I fear I can scarcely remember it."

The look on Sebastien's face translated to impatience.

"Let's start with your second question. I am, or once was, a member of the Svoda Gypsies. I left the island shortly before the mass exodus; you would have been but an infant at the time. More importantly, I am a Firemancer."

"You're Svoda? And a Firemancer?" Sebastien replied, shocked.

"And a dead one at that!" she added, her tone humored. "And for now, must stay so."

"Why? Why pretend you are dead?"

"Look into my eyes, Sebastien. I know you recognized them the moment you saw them."

Sebastien lost his breath. He could not speak, but only shake his head. He jumped up from the table and paced the room.

"You can't be!" he finally mustered out. "How?"

"It is a very long story. One I am not yet prepared to tell. Moreover, it is not why I called you here. I need your help. Help only you can give me, Sebastien."

"Why me? What help can I offer you? Why not go to her yourself? You're all she's ever wanted," he said, retaking his seat. "She's never admitted it, but I know."

"Which is why only you can help me, Sebastien. You know my daughter better than anyone. Except, perhaps Colin." She paused, biting her lip nervously. "There is something I need to show you."

"I'm sorry," Sebastien interrupted. "This is just... crazy! I mean, I can see it, yes, it's obvious. You are Meghan Jacoby's mother. She looks just like you. And she's a Firemancer, too!"

95

The woman's face looked sad, confused and anxious all at once.

"Believe me, Sebastien, when I say that what I have done, I have done for the greater good. I do one day hope to set things right. However, for now, there are things happening that are much larger than either you or me. Perhaps you need a different perspective," she said, breathing heavily. "You've spent your entire life as friends to Meghan and Colin. You never once told them about magic, even after magic came into their lives. Why?"

Sebastien slumped in his seat.

"Since I was little, I was told over and over again that they were special. That they needed protection. That they could not find out about magic, and if the time came when they did, I could not expose who I was. I was to be their friend. That's it." Sebastien's face ached with pain. "I never knew what was to happen. I had no idea what *special* meant until it was too late and they were gone. If I *had* known what kind of dangers they would be faced with, I might have chosen not to be so secretive," he admitted. "But at the time, I thought it was the right thing to do."

"Then you understand why *I* have done this terrible thing. My sacrifice has the potential to save countless innocent lives, Sebastien, including my daughter's. I have foreseen it! Besides, I am not the only one with secrets," she added with a wink. "I know more about you than you might think."

"I-I have to do what I can," he stammered. "To help them."

"Which takes us back to the reason I called you here. There is something I need you to see, Sebastien." She arose from the table. "Wait here, I'll be right back." She came back seconds later with a candle in the shape of Meghan Jacoby. She put the candle on the table and lit it.

"I must warn you, that what you are about to see might be difficult to stomach."

She proceeded to show him the future vision, in which Meghan killed Colin and Catrina.

When finished, Sebastien sat silently, stunned.

"Is that really what will happen?" he said after awhile.

"If we do not intervene, then yes. I am afraid that it will."

"I don't understand, though. How could Colin turn evil? He's so....NOT!" he said for lack of a better term.

"I have not been able to see what causes this path. Firemancy is not all seeing and all knowing. Helping my daughter is the most important thing I can do."

Sebastien noted something then. "So far, you keep talking about your daughter this and your daughter that. Have you no concern for your son, too? I will not allow him to turn evil."

"Oh. I surely hope that you can save Colin!" she said fervently. "Doing so will not only save lives, but prevent years of havoc and heartache!"

She stopped and looked into Sebastien's eyes.

"Colin Jacoby is not my son."

Sebastien nearly fell out of his chair. Of all the things this woman had told him, and shown him, this was the most shocking news of all.

"I am confused as to how it's believed that he is Meghan's twin. I honestly do not know who Colin Jacoby is, or where he comes from."

"But they can hear each others thoughts... finish each other's sentences... I was told they were discovered in the same crib at an orphanage."

"The orphanage is part of that long story I do not yet wish to tell," Meghan's mother spoke. "Perhaps there is some connection I am not yet aware of. Colin has some aura surrounding him. Something I cannot break through. I can only *see* him, when it involves Meghan. I have not been able to see his past, present or future, when she is not in the picture. It is something I have experienced only one time, previously," she added, as if she were not sure she wanted to continue.

"What do you mean?" Sebastien asked.

"I dare not speak it," she replied. "I am most likely wrong anyway," she added, standing up from the table. "Save your friends, Sebastien, and none of this will come to pass."

"What must I do?" he asked slowly.

"I need you to deliver something to my daughter."

"How? I would have to show myself to her. She would know there are other doorways. Other ways to come home."

"And I know why you are afraid of this truth. But we all must be willing to sacrifice for this cause."

She stood and took out a small white candle and handed it to him. She stroked his face lovingly.

"You have already sacrificed much for such a young life. Nevertheless, I must ask you to risk my daughter *never* forgiving you, in order to save her life. She will not be able to live if she kills Colin. Regardless of blood, he is her brother."

Sebastien took hold of the candle. "I've already betrayed her. Will it truly matter if she finds me out now, or later? I will have to face her someday." He sighed deeply. "You haven't by chance, happened to have seen if she forgives me or not, have you?" he asked nonchalantly.

"I am sorry. It is a future still undetermined. I will say this. I do hope that she does. My daughter deserves someone as smart, compassionate and courageous as you, Sebastien Jendaya."

He stood up from the table as well.

"What do I do with this candle? Just hand it over?"

"You will deliver it, and you'll know when the time is right to do so, and she will know what to do with it. Meghan is a Firemancer after all."

"Maybe someday, she'll forgive me for the secrets I hid from her. But *not* telling her you're alive…"

"I know. And for asking it of you, I am truly sorry for what it might mean."

Sebastien nodded, and departed. There was another stop he needed to make, before beginning this new quest.

##

Meghan and Juliska studied quietly in the candle room. A strange scratching sound startled Meghan and she jumped, when Pajak, Juliska's pet spider, scratched and clinked its way by her, crawling up Juliska's dress, coming to a rest on her shoulder.

"Ah, my pet. Good hunting?"

The spider touched one of its glassy feet to her chin. Juliska's eyes widened, as if the spider had told her interesting news.

"Let's take a lunch break," Juliska decided. "After, Meghan, I want you to practice on your own, and then later tonight we'll do some more hands on practice together."

Meghan did not wish to leave the candle room. It already felt like home and she desired greatly to make her own. Nevertheless, she obligingly stowed her study supplies and grabbed her book. She gently awoke Nona, as she had fallen asleep while watching Meghan study. Nona jumped to the ready and waited for Meghan by the door.

"It's so hideous!" Nona heard Meghan's thoughts betray. "Can she actually talk with that thing?"

"Is it so hard to believe that Pajak can talk?" Meghan heard Nona reply.

Meghan smiled at her loyal Catawitch. "No, I guess not. But even on your worst day, I'd take you a thousand times over, versus Pajak!"

"I'll take that as a compliment," Nona said, stepping out of the candle room and into Juliska's room.

"See you later," Meghan said, as she passed Juliska, exiting as well.

Juliska nodded, but was too engrossed in her conversation with Pajak to speak aloud. As she exited, Meghan heard high-pitched squeaking and chirping, and then heard Juliska reply.

"Oh, really, did he? How very interesting, my pet. Very good job," she spoke.

"Apparently they cannot hear each others' thoughts, like we can," Meghan noted, adding, "I wonder how one learns to speak spider?"

For some reason Nona found Meghan's comment funny and laughed in a raucous, cat-like manner. The more Meghan thought about it, it was a little funny, thinking of someone learning to speak spider.

It felt good to laugh. It also helped that spotty beams of sun were sneaking through the clouds and warming the meadow. Overall, the mood seemed more cheerful than it had in the previous days.

"You know, Nona, it might actually come in handy to speak spider," Meghan said unexpectedly.

"How so?"

"It is not the first time Pajak has disappeared for hours, only to come back and have something it wants to discuss with Juliska."

"And it's obviously a conversation she wants to have in private," Nona added, understanding Meghan's concern at once. "Maybe I'll have to add keeping an eye on Pajak to my list of duties..." her thoughts wandered off as she caught the whiff of a rodent nearby.

"See you after lunch," Meghan whispered, as Nona vaulted in the opposite direction.

Meghan made a point to pass by Billie's, so she could see if Colin wanted to join her. Her visit proved timely, as Billie stepped out just as she was about to enter. Colin followed behind her. *Billie looks a bit pale*, she noted.

"Ah, the sister," Billie spoke. Her voice lacked the usual passion and fervor. "How are you finding yourself, Meghan Jacoby?"

"Oh, um, fine I guess."

Billie nodded and sauntered off toward the cantina.

"What's up with Billie?" Meghan asked Colin.

"We're a little worried about her. We think she knows someone in the missing caravan. We think she's really worried."

Meghan could not help but notice Colin's use of the word 'we' and to her surprise, she felt a twinge of jealousy. *We* always used to be the term associated with her and Colin. Now, it appeared, Catrina had replaced her in that role.

Colin checked that the coast was clear and held the door open for Catrina. Though she could not see her, Meghan was sure to whisper hello.

"She says hi back," Colin smiled.

"Heading to eat, you want to join me?" asked Meghan.

"We were heading there, too."

Upon arrival, they glanced for Jae, but their luck did not hold as he did not appear to be eating lunch just then. They located the jutting rocks at the edge of the meadow, so they could eat with less of a chance of someone overhearing.

People were quieter than normal, and the main topic of conversation stemmed around the hunting party. They were still missing.

During lunch, the cloud cover returned, cooling the air. Soon, patches of fog lined the meadow and the edge of the woods surrounding it. This turn in the weather matched the turn of the mood, as more people arrived to eat, and the conversations turned to hushed whispers that only those close by could hear.

It was clear that most everyone felt sure that something sinister had befallen the hunting party. This, combined with the already missing caravan, left little hope that something terrible would not befall them all.

As people arrived to get food, they ignored acquaintances they might normally speak to, and avoided sitting with anyone they did not consider close friends or family. Those already eating watched the new arrivals with paranoid glances. Many of those glances made their way to Meghan. It seemed as though every time she lifted her head to look at something, someone's eyes were darting away, pretending they had not been staring.

"Kind of losing my appetite," Meghan said after a bit. She had eaten about half of her food. "This place is starting to give me the creeps."

"Catrina agrees," Colin replied softly. "And for that matter, so do I."

"Here, take the rest of my food. I can't finish." Meghan wrapped her half-eaten meat pie in a napkin and handed it to him.

Colin put it in his pocket to eat later.

"I think I'm doing the opposite of what you need right now, Colin. Drawing way too much attention our way."

"Yeah, what's with all the staring?" he asked. He turned, to where Meghan assumed Catrina was sitting, and nodded understandingly. "They're waiting for you to have some kind of vision, aren't they?" he said, answering his own question.

"I guess," Meghan replied. "You know, someday, I would really enjoy just a few hours when I'm not being stared at!" She folded her arms and set her chin in resigned acceptance.

As the crowd continued to grow, space became tight, and people started sitting closer together and inevitably, talking. Heated conversations began sprouting throughout the cantina, table by table. To the twins, the noise helped lift the dreariness of the clouds and fog, as well as sidetrack them from their worries.

Suddenly, a scream echoed through the meadow, silencing all debates. No one spoke, but most stood and searched for the source of the scream.

It came from a little girl.

She pointed toward the woods with a look of terror on her face.

Everyone froze.

There was movement at the edge of the meadow.

The twins' first thoughts strayed to the Scratchers. This could not be them, though, as they would have attacked from the air.

"Don't let go," Colin whispered to Catrina, not wanting to lose her if they had to make a sudden escape. She took a firm hold of his sweater and held her breath in nervous anticipation, just the same as everyone else.

Branches broke under approaching footsteps.

Trees and shrubs rustled as someone, or something, disturbed them by walking through.

Balaton came running to the front of the group, with belts slung over their shoulders, ready for a battle if it came to it.

Meghan and Colin repeatedly thought they saw movement, but each time their eyes caught something, it disappeared just as quickly.

Jae popped in alongside Meghan, glaring menacingly across the edge of the meadow.

The crowd gasped in unison as shadows emerged from the trees, taking the form of people. And yet, they seemed to disappear and blend in with their background. Soon, they had surrounded the entire meadow.

A firm voice spoke.

"We do not mean to cause alarm. We come only to speak to your leader, regarding an urgent matter."

Meghan and Colin were surprised when Garner Sadorus stepped forward, rather than Juliska Blackwell.

"Show yourselves if you mean no ill will!" he demanded. Garner once again wore his boisterous overcoat. Although the weather seemed more appropriate now, with the sudden chill expanding across the meadow.

The leader of the new arrivals stepped out of the shadows and into the meadow.

The Svoda gasped in unison.

"Stripers!" someone nearby said.

At first glance, they appeared human, but upon closer inspection, the twins noticed stripes of what appeared to be lizard-like skin running down their arms and necks. It seemed odd that in the chilly air, they wore only minimal clothing.

"Are they...human?" asked Colin.

Jae leaned in, whispering to the twins. "Do you remember in the retelling festival, that there was a boat lost at sea during the battle, and all were assumed dead?"

They nodded yes.

"Well, the story doesn't add that many years later, it was discovered they had survived."

"Survived? That's good, isn't it?" asked Meghan.

"Yes, and kind of no," said Jae, while shrugging.

"Why don't they look like you then?" asked Colin.

"Short version: A long time ago they befriended a group of animal magicians known as chameleons, and in return, they were given some of their magic. It changed them. Made them more than human."

Colin breathed out fast, not able to hide his shock.

The leader approached Garner, but he spoke as if talking to everyone in the meadow.

"We have come because we are hunting something. Something evil. Something that must be destroyed!"

The Svoda remained paralyzed and could only stare at the Stripers in awe and fear.

"What is it you hunt?" asked Garner.

The leader of the Stripers glanced around the meadow, as if seeking out this terrible evil amongst the Svoda.

"I see you have nearly cleaned up the devastation that was cast upon this place."

At this moment, Juliska Blackwell appeared and took over from Garner. He took a few steps back, remaining close.

"What do you know of it?" demanded Juliska.

"And you would be?" the leader asked.

Juliska did not reply immediately. Her face studied the Stripers closely. After a tense minute, she finally broke her silence.

"I am Juliska Nandalia Blackwell, Queen of the Svoda Gypsies. And you would be?"

A sinister smile spread over the Striper's face.

"I am KarNavan. And most pleased to make the acquaintance of a Queen." He bowed his head, as if paying her respect, but something about his actions hinted that his respect was artificial.

"Again, I ask you. What do you know of the condition of this meadow?"

KarNavan's face wrestled to keep its smile. "We came across this meadow in its current state, a full evening before you arrived."

Jae stomped his foot onto the ground. "They know we've been here, the entire time."

"They've must have been spying," Meghan said.

It appeared as though many Svoda were under the same belief, as their fearful stares now turned to angry glares.

"And you saw no one?" questioned Juliska.

"Not one single living person," KarNavan replied. "Just belongings and smoldering fires." He paused. "If I have concluded correctly, there are people missing? And these people are your kin?"

"You are correct in that assumption," Juliska replied.

The angry glares of the Svoda now dissolved into bitter disappointment, as once again, the search for their loved ones seemed to be at another dead end.

"I am sorry that I cannot assist you with your missing kin. Perhaps I can bring you *some* good news..." He snapped his fingers and out of the woods trudged the missing hunting party.

Cries of relief spread and friends and family raced forward to welcome home their missing loved ones.

"We got lost," said one of the hunters. "Our magic gave out and we just couldn't find the way back to the meadow. We walked around lost for days, until the Stripers found us."

The leader of the party whispered to Garner as he passed by him.

"We told them nothing, except who we are and that we were hunting."

Garner nodded that he understood.

"Thank you for returning our hunting party. We feared the worst," Juliska told the Stripers. "With that appreciation in mind, shall we get to the point of your visit? You know better than I that your reputation is not built upon trust and kindness."

KarNavan's menacing smile returned.

"We realize our reputation precedes us, our work is sometimes cutthroat in nature," his eyes narrowed in shrewd pleasure. "But we ask for peace, for now we fight a common enemy! We were once brothers. Let us be brothers once again."

"You wish us to make peace?" Juliska's voice mocked. "You pursue treasure at the bequest of the highest bidder, and as you say, your cutthroat methods are well known."

"I wonder," whispered Jae, "if they only kept the hunters alive to more easily enter our camp?"

Meghan and Colin gulped, their throats feeling dry and hard.

"So this is what you mean by 'yes, and kinda no,'" said Colin. "Good that they survived, but bad, because they turned into maniacal treasure hunters?"

Jae's reply was a low snarl.

Speaking of non-human behavior. Both twins had thought it at the same time and caught each other's eye. Catrina even recognized that the sound that came from Jae was not normal.

To further their surprise, Viancourt member Tanzea Chase suddenly wobbled up beside Jae, touching his arm. She shot him a look the twins did not comprehend. But Jae nodded to her, clearly understanding.

KarNavan stole back the twins' attention as he jumped up onto a rock, so to better see everyone in the meadow.

"The enemy we seek is one of you!"

The crowd gasped, aghast at the charge.

"What is the meaning of this?" Garner shouted.

Juliska raised her hand to calm him. She turned back to KarNavan.

"I ask the same question. What is the meaning of this charge?"

"The enemy we seek is not only an enemy to us, but to all that live in the magical and non-magical world," he began. "A child. A child that will one day become a *Projector*..."

The crowd had no response but silence, as they were overcome with disbelief.

"This is not possible. Projectors died out long ago," insisted Juliska.

"What I believe you mean to say is, were *killed* off long ago. Regardless of this point, I unfortunately speak the truth. We have been tracking the magic of this child Projector for the last few months. We were finally able to track the location. It brought us here."

Panic ensued.

The Svoda began looking around at each child, wondering which unlucky soul it could be. It seemed the Stripers had no idea.

"Maybe the child caused this devastation!" a voice shouted.

"Yes! It's not one of ours! It must've been from the other group," someone shouted.

"Calm yourselves!" Juliska forcefully told her people, before they could say more. "While I believe that the existence of a Projector is not possible," she continued, aiming her words at the Stripers, "I must ask, what are your plans? Once you find this child?"

KarNavan cast his gaze over the people. He avoided the Banon's question.

"We will leave you now, to think about what we have told you. We will return."

The Stripers walked out of the meadow, melting into the woods.

"How do we know they actually left, since they can blend in?" asked Meghan.

"We don't," answered Jae, darkly.

The group waited for their Banon to speak. Once she felt it safe to do so, she made only a quick statement.

"I will take the information we've just heard under council of the Viancourt. Balaton, keep your perimeters under constant surveillance."

The Balaton scurried to keep guard of the meadow's borders.

"Garner, bring me the leader of the hunting party. I wish to speak with him. Darius, Tanzea, please wait for me in my tent."

Garner dashed away to locate the leader of the hunting party, while Darius and Tanzea worked their way across the meadow to Juliska's tent.

"As for everyone else, at this time nothing has changed. Attend to your duties! Until we can either prove or deny this Projector claim, we must be vigilant. Keep your eyes and ears open!"

Juliska nodded toward Meghan, beckoning her.

"Gotta run!" Meghan said.

The crowd dispersed slowly, eyeing each other more so now than ever before. Especially the children. Some had looks of despair. Some, anger and bewilderment.

Irving Mochrie shouted for Jae to follow him. He did so, begrudgingly.

Colin had hoped he would have a few minutes alone with Jae, so he could ask him what he knew about Projectors, as Colin knew nothing.

When Colin and the invisible Catrina, arrived back at Billie's tent, he was surprised to see her home, sitting in the front room.

"What terrible times to be alive," she said. Her voice sounded hollow.

Colin sat down across from her, knowing that Catrina would sit on the ground close by and listen.

"What exactly is a Projector?" asked Colin.

"A poor, helpless creature with no choice but to accept its terrible fate," Billie answered.

Colin had expected bad, but the way Billie spoke, it was as if there was simply no hope.

"Projectors were thought to have died out long ago," she continued, her energy returning. "To be more correct, as the Striper said, were killed off long ago."

"Why?" asked Colin.

"Projectors, as children, are much like any other child. However, as they age, they change. They will become evil. They cannot stop it! Even if as a child they were a saint, their fate is sealed!"

Billie stood up now, invigorated by her story.

"Once a Projector reaches maturity, at age seventeen, magic turns on them like an infectious disease."

"What happens exactly? Do they turn seventeen and just start killing people?" Colin asked.

"I am afraid it is rather more complex than just killin'. A Projector's magic has *no* boundaries. *No* limitations. It is more magic than any *human* can control. It can fulfill any whim in the blink of an eye. An entire village could be wiped out of existence. An entire landscape completely changed. A Projector will destroy everything they love, touch or even think about, without the most careful control. Control that's just not possible for a human mind. This... this is why they are searched out and killed without mercy."

"Wow," was the only response he could muster. It did not seem to do this news justice.

"Wow indeed young Mr. Jacoby. Wow indeed," Billie agreed.

Colin glanced at Catrina. She, however, did not look as astonished at this information as he did. *She must have already known this, like everyone else.*

"It could literally be any child," Billie told him. "Even a child that's been deemed something else, like your sister being a Firemancer. Not that it's her of course, just an example," Billie said with more of her normal vigor. "The signs start coming on stronger in the teen years."

"What kind of signs?" Colin asked.

"It can be different for each child, but in general, their nature will start to change. The nicest person will suddenly become mean, cunning or vengeful. There will be an increase of magical accidents. Unexplainable happenings."

"Like the devastation in the meadow?" he asked.

"Perhaps, although I feel not likely. The devastation in the meadow has a more physical cause behind it."

Colin let out a long sigh.

"Chances are that this child doesn't even know what they are. If what the Stripers say is true though, and they did track a real Projector's magic here…" Billie did not finish and her stare gazed over to the trunk she had dragged in from the meadow.

"I can't imagine," Colin started then stopped. "I can't imagine what it would be like to find out *you* are that child. Finding out you have no future. No chance. Or that if you lived you would destroy everything or anyone you cared about."

"It is a terrible fate," fretted Catrina, looking away.

She turned her head to hide the tears falling down her cheeks. He wanted to comfort her, but could not with Billie in the room.

"A horrendous tragedy for any family," Billie added. "There are tales of families going on the run, trying to protect their child, blind to the horrors to come, only to fall prey to the uncontrollable magic, or to be killed alongside the child."

They sat in silence for a while.

Colin tried to picture the faces of the children he had gone to school with in Grimble, or seen walking around the camp. Was it one of them? More likely than not, the child belonged to the missing caravan.

Had that child unknowingly caused the devastation? If so, what had happened to all those Svoda? Were they dead? Lost? Or had some other tragedy befallen them? Could the Stripers themselves have had something to do with their disappearance?

Catrina sniffled.

Glass Coffin. Left behind in a sleep she wasn't meant to awaken from. Could she...

Colin blocked those thoughts, infuriated that he even dared think it.

He arose in a huff and entered his room.

He held open the door long after he was through.

This time Billie noticed.

He had not been careful.

He let the canvas door fall shut, hoping she would not think too much of it.

##

Meghan arrived alongside Juliska at her tent. The Viancourt, along with Pantin Hollee, were already seated at the table awaiting the Banon's arrival.

"Please feel free to wait for me in my room. I will be along shortly," Juliska told Meghan.

Meghan, having no desire to be in the same room as Garner Sadorus or mothball lady, obliged without question. Nona joined Meghan moments later.

"I guess we can still hear what goes on outside this room," she said.

"Hadn't thought of that," Meghan whispered. "Guess I don't need to whisper, seeing as they cannot hear us. Still, it just seems strange that we can hear them just a few feet away, and yet if I were to shout, they would not hear it."

"Lets not test that theory right now," suggested Nona, tuning into the conversation now beginning in the front room.

"Sounds heated," Meghan added.

They heard the voice of Darius Hadrian.

"I fear the Striper speaks the truth. Nevertheless, history proves they cannot be trusted. There may well be a Projector, but I doubt they are telling us everything."

"If there is indeed a Projector, we must find out what the Stripers' plans are once they locate this child," insisted Garner. "Ending the life of this Projector should at least be done mercifully. If they capture this child, it would no doubt suffer greatly."

Meghan had difficulty believing that the compassionate words she was hearing were coming from Garner Sadorus. Then, as with so many things in this new life, her attitude changed as she questioned the use of the word compassionate, as they still spoke of ending a child's life.

"Idiots have tried to harness a Projector's power before," added Tanzea, her voice sounding aged and tired. "Sure enough, they'll try again."

"Which we all know is a terrible mistake," Juliska spoke. "But I agree, with all your points. We do not know the entire story. The child *will* suffer at their hands. And yet, its fate is predetermined. It must die."

"If I may," said Garner. "We should focus on discovering more about the Striper's plans. Who hired them, for starters?"

"How do you propose we do such a thing?" asked Tanzea.

"Yes, *how* is the real question," agreed Juliska. "We are in unfamiliar territory. And for some unexplained reason, our magic is greatly weakened here."

"And diminishing more each day," added Hollee.

"Surely your visions are not, though," said Hadrian.

"No. They are fine," lied Juliska with ease. "Unfortunately, none of them are being... helpful at the moment. Besides, Darius, you know they don't work like that."

"Of course, Banon. My apologies. These circumstances are complicated. I certainly do not wish to add to that complication."

"If I see anything of value or understanding, you know the court will be the first to know."

Meghan began to understand just how important Juliska's visions were to the safety of her people.

Nona put a paw on her leg, comforting her.

"I still have so much to learn, Nona."

"Then I will help you study."

Meghan nodded and read aloud to Nona, hoping to retain as much knowledge as possible.

##

Sebastien Jendaya arrived home in the Northern Maine woods. He stood in front of two ancient white pine trees. From where he stood, the thick forest continued as far as his eyes could see. However, upon stepping through the two white pines, he stepped into a different world. A bustling village nestled amongst the trees.

This village had been his home since his parents had been banished, nearly thirteen years prior, from the Svoda Island off the northern Maine shores.

Sebastien hustled down a pathway and then climbed a staircase, which went to a bridge high above the ground, connecting from tree to tree. He stopped in front of a door but stopped himself before entering. He felt nervous being home. He took a deep breath and entered.

"Sebastien! You're home!" his father, Milo, exclaimed. "Kay," he shouted, while hugging his son. Kay Jendaya's small frame emerged from another room. She rushed forward to hold her son close.

"You have been gone for so long," his mother cried.

"Oh, don't cry, Mom. I'm fine. Everything is going perfect," he insisted.

"I just worry so," she mumbled.

"We're your parents, it's what we do," Milo reminded. "It's nice to have you home, Son. C'mon in and sit. Rest. I'm sure you have lots to tell."

"Yes. Sit. Relax. I'll make a bite to eat," said Kay, darting into the kitchen.

Sebastien grimaced. He knew he would have to keep most of his actions secret. If not his work for Amelia, then his visit with Meghan's very much alive mother.

"I'll send a leaf to Amelia," Milo said. "She'll want to know you're home."

His mother exited the kitchen with a tall stack of sandwiches.

"Sorry, this is all I could whip up quickly."

Sebastien licked his lips and grabbed two. "I sure do miss home cooked food," he said, grabbing a third.

"Well, we'll have some time now. I'll cook you all the real food you can eat," his mother said.

Sebastien dropped the third sandwich, looking guilty.

"You're not staying long? Are you?" asked Milo.

Sebastien's eyes answered their question.

"We'll just have to make due with the time we have then," his mother insisted, trying to sound happy. "You know how proud we are of you, right?"

"Yeah, I know, Mom."

"We could not have asked for a better, more loyal son. We are so very proud of the work you're doing."

"I still worry, though," his mother added. "I just cannot help it. You're still just my little boy," she said, her eyes getting teary. "We all have our jobs to do. I just wish yours would keep you a little closer to home."

"Whatever your next job is, just be careful. Okay, Son?" Milo ordered.

"Sure, dad. Always!" he replied.

He really wanted to burst. To shout his news that Meghan's mother was still alive. To tell them everything he had been up to. But he bit his lip and kept quiet. They could not know. And neither could Amelia.

##

"Father!" said Colby, startled. "I was expecting the new teacher."

"Little fact I forgot to mention," he informed his son. "I am your new teacher."

Colby twisted in his seat with anticipation. Lessons with his father were always the best ones.

"What kind of magic are we going to learn today?" Colby asked him eagerly.

Jurekai's gaunt smile lifted to one corner.

"No magic today," he answered. He saw his son's heart sink. "Today, my son, I have decided it is time for you to know where we came from. How we came to be. For as you know, we were not always the Grosvenor."

Colby's sinking heart leapt. This is a story he had always wanted to hear, but his father always refused to tell. Colby's desk vanished and the room began to darken. The walls began to lighten, their stained glass windows shimmering to life with color and movement.

"Mother," Fazendiin called out.

The silhouette of his mother appeared in the stained glass.

"Would you mind, please, to tell the story?" he asked her kindly.

"So it shall be, my son," she replied.

The picture in the stained glass shifted as she began to speak. Beams of light emanated and danced around the room, throwing shadows.

"In the beginning of the earth, magic flowed as naturally as breathing through all living things."

The scene changed to a field, with plants, trees, animals and humans all living together in peace.

"But as with any world," she continued, "there were periods of conflict and war. One such war changed the landscape of the world, forever."

The picture of a man materialized in the stained glass, standing alongside what appeared to be a large cow.

"The man you see here is named Babiin Balick, in his day, a known fool of a farmer. Today, he is remembered for an accidental discovery which forever changed the world of magic."

The scene in the glass turned gruesome, as it showed Babiin slaughtering the cow-like animal, reaching into the dying creature's body, extracting something.

"The Mazuruk: A beast relative to the modern day cow. In its day, this beast was used much as it is today, for milk, meat and clothing. One day, upon slaughtering a Mazaruk, while it was yet alive, a stone fell out of its third stomach. Babiin picked up the glass-like stone and put it in his pocket, never giving it a second thought."

Colby watched the stained glass intently, not wanting to miss any part. With each new part his grandmother spoke, the colors in the stained glass shifted, creating a new picture.

"As the days passed, Babiin noticed a change. He was stronger. His magical abilities and strength were growing. At the same time, concerns in his village arose, as other peoples magic weakened. Nothing like this had ever occurred before. Weeks after he had taken the Mazaruk's stone, it dawned on Babiin that his increase of power had begun after he had put the stone in his pocket. He tested his theory by burying the stone far away from his home. Almost instantly, the further away he got from the stone, the more weakened he became. He dug up the stone and just as instantly, grew stronger."

Colby sat on the edge of his seat while listening intently. His father had only recently mentioned the subject of something called a Mazy Stone. But had not told him any more. He kept his attention on the story.

"What Babiin did not realize, was that the increase in his power was not only aided by the stone, but that the stone increased his power by stealing magical energy from the living things nearby, weakening other's magic. For months, he researched and tested the Stone's powers. The most important discovery, beyond weakening other's magical powers, is that the magic could be transferred out of the stone and into a living person, thus permanently making this person stronger."

Stronger? He knew his father was strong, and old, but now, he wondered just how old. It was something they had never discussed. His father's skin was leather-like, gaunt and thin. Yet his mind was sharp. Perhaps he was finally about to find out just how old his father truly was.

"Pay attention, Colby," his father scolded, seeing Colby's attention wander. He missed nothing.

Fazediin's mother continued her story.

"After learning everything he could about the Stones, Babiin's hunger intensified. Not just for more power, but for money. He realized his discovery would be worth a lot, to the right buyer. Babiin also worried that the damage he had caused in his own village would be found out, so he fled. But not before slaughtering every last Mazuruk he owned, and seizing the stones from their dying bodies."

The stained glass picture now morphed into a map, focusing in on a part of the map noted as Shogharne Territory. As the territory came into better view, it stopped in a village set near the edge of a vast mountain.

"Babiin traveled to the Shogharne Territory seeking out a clan he had heard rumor of... one that was infamous for their unending search for immortality. They were called Vetala: Energy Vampires. Their ability to extract and consume the life force from living things allowed them extended life. But not the immortality they desired, as the results were not permanent and the ability declined with age."

Colby's thoughts reeled with this information. *Father told me once he was descended from a Vetala clan. Does this mean I am a vampire, like in the story? Or am I an immortal, like my father? Or am I some kind of hybrid? My mother is just a human... from a magical bloodline, but just human...*

Colby had always wanted to know the answers to these questions; however, his father had repeatedly told him that this knowledge was something he would learn at the appropriate time. Did his father think now was the appropriate time?

"Babiin approached the clan leader," the story went on, "asking him what he would be willing to pay for limitless magic. This clan leader scoffed at Babiin's claims. This leader knew there could be no such thing, as his clan had been searching for hundreds of years to no avail. If there had been such a thing, they would have discovered it themselves.

"To prove what he said, Babiin left one Stone in the hands of the clan leader, insisting he test the Stone's ability. Babiin told the leader where they could locate him once his claim was proven true. The leader, in return, told Babiin that if the Stone did not perform as promised, he would not step off Shogharne Territory, alive.

"Babiin had nothing to fear. Within a day, the clan leader realized the power of Babiin's Stone and sought him out. However, the clan leader had no intention of buying the Stones.

"The clan leader forced Babiin to tell him everything he knew about the Stones, or face instant death. He surrendered all knowledge without hesitation, and for this, the clan leader spared his life."

The stained glass morphed again, this time, unraveling a horrific scene: A bloody and terrifying massacre.

"In the weeks that followed, the clan leader ordered the slaughter of every Mazaruk in the surrounding villages, for each single Stone had a limit on how much magical energy it could contain. Therefore, the more Stones one possessed, the stronger one could become. Thousands of Stones were collected from these beasts, and with them, the Vetala collected power. More power than they had ever thought possible.

"Unknowing villagers suspected nothing. The Vetala appeared as travelers, just passing through. It was at first feared that some terrible plague was to blame, as village after village discovered their magic was weakened, and then one day, completely gone. The Stones left everything in their wake alive, but powerless and magic-less.

"This is when the Vetala clan made a disastrous error. They grew arrogant, allowing someone to discover their secret. The news spread like wild fire and soon, any village that still retained their magical powers began executing Mazuruk, in hopes of defending themselves in the battle that would inevitably follow."

Colby had a thousand questions he wanted to shout, but knew his father would not approve. His eyes never left the stained glass, where the pictures continued to shift and change.

"Over the months that followed, this news spread across the magical world like a disease. At the height of this massacre, nearly every Mazuruk had been exterminated, and you had either lost your magical powers to someone possessing a Stone, or possessed enough Stones to steal other people's powers.

"Wars broke out all over the world, village against village, clan against clan. Those with the Stones, kept the power. The Shogharne clan still possessed the largest number of these Stones."

She stopped for a moment as the stained glass darkened and then lightened again, once more displaying a scene with Babiin Balick.

"Seeing the destruction his discovery had caused, Babiin spent the remainder of his life making amends for his actions. He created a group of warriors that wandered the earth for many years, painstakingly collecting and destroying the stones, and those that used them for harm.

"But it was during this time that nine of the most powerful Vetala learned an awesome truth: The Mazuruk Stones could give them the immortality they had so long desired. Using their innate powers as Energy Vampires, they could combine the magical energies from a single Stone, into another, fusing them together. They did this with hundreds of Stones, until they had built a Stone large enough to contain the magical energy required for immortality.

"Babiin Balick and his followers learned of this plan too late. They set out to stop it, but fate had determined otherwise. The nine remaining Vetala from the Shogharne Territory, simply needed to touch the Stone simultaneously, and its power would be permanently fused with their own, filling their life force completely."

At this point Jurekai Fazendiin's mother stopped and looked at him, as if to ask if she should continue.

"Yes, Mother," he told her. "If I want the truth known, I want the entire truth known."

She nodded and began to speak again.

"The Immortality Stone was hidden, its location only known by the nine, to ensure that it could not be destroyed. For if it was destroyed... their immortality, and thus their lives, would end."

Colby breathed out in disbelief. He had known his father was immortal, but could his immortality end? Did this also mean that his father was one of the nine original immortals? He had often heard of him spoken as *the original*... if this were true, Colby again desired greatly to know how this affected his own life. Nevertheless, he waited, knowing the story was not yet finished.

"The immortals made the choice to go into hiding, allowing the rest of the world to wage their war. Babiin Balick continued to wage his own war, which lasted long beyond his death. Eventually, after many years, his followers tracked down and destroyed the remaining Mazuruk Stones. There were unexpected casualties, however. The biggest being the near eradication of magic. The next being that the battle had lasted so many years, that new generations had been born and died, having no knowledge of magic.

"The world was changed, magic no longer at the forefront of everyday life. As time passed, so did the knowledge of what once was. The few remaining humans that still held onto their magical powers feared for their lives, as magic became myth. Which when happened upon, was reviled as evil to be purged from the earth.

"In order to better their odds of survival, the smaller magical clans joined forces. You will know them today as the Svoda Gypsies. Many of Babiin Balick's followers' descendents make up a good portion of the Gypsies members. His own bloodline remains true to his cause, still today."

Jurekai interrupted his mother's story at this point. "It was Babiin's own son that cursed my mother's soul," he added. "Cursed her to live without a physical body, so very, very long ago."

"But father," Colby interrupted, "with all your power and knowledge, you could not find a way to free her?"

"Not yet, Son. Please finish Mother, so that he knows everything."

"About two hundred years ago, the very Stone that gave the nine immortals their power was discovered and stolen by the descendents of Babiin Balick. They tried to destroy the Stone, to no avail. Then, it was stolen again, by one of the last living Projectors. One of the few able to tame the power, for he was more than human, and a human mind is not capable of controlling that sort of power. He made claim that the Stone could not only heal an uncontrollable Projector's powers, but that it could also be made to either heal or destroy all remaining magic."

Colby's father interrupted. "Whoever controls the Immortality Stone, controls *everything*, Son." He nodded to his mother to finish her story.

"The Projector who made these claims hid the Stone. It has not yet been located. It is believed that he left vital clues to the Stone's location in a book called the Magicante, a book that was written by this Projector. After his death, about fifty years later, the book disappeared from all knowledge."

"That is," interrupted Jurekai Fazendiin again, "until it popped into the hands of a young boy, Colin Jacoby."

So this is why my father wants that book so badly. Colby finally knew why he had been seeking out this book.

"What you must take from all of this my son," his father said, "is that the Magicante is a vital piece of the puzzle. It will lead us to the Stone. Without this Stone, my immortality is at stake. Without this Stone, our legacy is at stake. Without this Stone, we cannot live in peace, as in the wrong hands, this Stone could be made to destroy *all* magic... including ours. We can be overthrown. We are not invincible."

Colby was beginning to comprehend just how old his father truly was. And now he knew that his father could die... but again, what did this mean for him?

"There is one other point you must understand, my son. *I* was the clan leader that Babiin Balick approached so very long ago. It was *I* that discovered our path to immortality. I will not allow all I have worked for all these years to be undone! With the Magicante I can find the Stone. With the Stone, I can control all magic. With the Stone, I can remain immortal, forever. Alas, I am not an ignorant man. And this... this is why I brought you into the world."

Colby could not speak. He could scarcely catch his breath.

"You are descended from an immortal bloodline. My bloodline. The most powerful ever to exist. Your birth guarantees that a Fazendiin will remain, even if my life is ended."

"What do you mean?" Colby asked.

"A child born to one of the nine immortals would be passed on this immortality through the blood, making them a true immortal. You, my son, cannot die."

A million questioned rushed through his brain.

Can't die! But I'm aging... will that stop at some point? If we find the stone, will I be the

most powerful person in the entire world? Will I
control everything? If I am injured, will I just
heal?

The stained glass window returned to its original form.

"Thank you, Mother," Fazendiin spoke softly.

He turned his attention back to Colby.

"There is no one else like you in this, or any other world, my son. Your potential is limitless. But, you are still young, and have much to learn. I will not have any son of mine, no matter how powerful he will become, live in ignorance or arrogance. I made that mistake once, and look at what happened to this world."

"Yes, Father," was all Colby could respond.

"I will make you a king, my son. You will become my greatest achievement."

Chapter Five

Dew blanketed the meadow, casting glistening shadows upon the trees as the sun beamed down. A full day had passed since the Stripers had arrived and made their claim that a child Projector was somewhere nearby.

Meghan met up with Colin and Catrina and headed for breakfast. On their way, she described a vivid dream she'd had the night before.

"I think I was hearing Colby's thought's," she said after awhile. "Or maybe I was seeing bits of his dreams. I still don't know why I can do that, but it's so strange that the subject of my dream was Projectors, and we are now possibly dealing with one. Plus, he is not giving up his quest for your book, Colin. I wish my dream would have told me why!" she added in frustration. "Of course, I don't even know if what I dreamt is actually real."

Colin leaned into Catrina, whose voice only he could hear.

"Really?" said Colin. "That is definitely strange."

"What?" Meghan asked, annoyed. She wondered if this was how she and Colin had always come across when they would have secret conversations around Sebastien. She now understood why he would get irritated when they did it.

"Catrina says the details in your dream, regarding how the Grosvenor came to be, are accurate, according to what she has heard."

"How would she know? In my dream, this seemed like very privileged information," Meghan relayed to her brother. She also recalled reading in a schoolbook that it was unknown as to how the Grosvenor came to be. She did not get an answer as Jae came running up to them, appearing distressed.

"You guys haven't seen Corny have you?" he asked.

"Corny? No." said Colin.

"Thought he never came out of the dark?" Meghan added.

"Usually doesn't. I went to give him breakfast this morning and he wasn't in his room. Mom's worried, so I told her I'd look around."

"We can help if you want," offered Meghan. "I hope he didn't get confused and wander off into the woods."

"If he did, we'll never find him," worried Jae.

"Um. Guys. Search over!" Colin said, pointing.

Corny Tibbett shuffled his way into the camp cantina.

He searched the crowd, his eyes stopping on Colin Jacoby. He trudged his way over to Colin, ignoring both Jae and Meghan.

His grizzled face looked pale, even underneath the layers of tangled facial hair. Then, surprising everyone in the camp, Corny did something he had not done in many a long year. He spoke.

"I just wanted to see... one time... for myself." His voice sounded weak. His gaze wandered to the empty space next to Colin, in which the invisible Catrina Flummer stood.

Colin panicked.

Can he see her? Is the spell not working?

Corny took hold of Colin's shoulders, his eyes casting between him and the invisible Catrina.

"Hope or death?" Corny asked in a whisper only they could hear.

Colin did not respond. His mouth fell open, as if to try, but nothing came out. He did not know what Corny meant or how to respond. Corny let go of Colin and backed up a step.

"My part in this play is now finished," he muttered.

Corny Tibbett closed his eyes and slumped to the ground. Dead.

Colin, Catrina, Meghan and Jae just stared at his body in disbelief, almost expecting him to get back up again. Surely he could not die, just like that.

A crowd gathered around his body, wondering what to do. Corny had no actual family to contact. The Mochries were the closest thing he had. In just minutes, Balaton arrived to file a report on what had happened and carried away the body.

It did not take long for them to close the report.

"Poor, crazy old man," one of the Balaton spoke. "I knew him many years ago, when I was just a young boy before he lost his family. He was a kind man. Such a shame to see him this way. Although, I guess dying of old age is better than some of the other alternatives…" He followed his fellow Balaton out of the cantina.

"Please pass my condolences to Jae," Catrina whispered to Colin. "I know they were not really close, but his family did provide him a home for a long time."

Colin passed along her message, adding his own as well.

Inwardly, he felt bad for never making good on his promise to do something nice for Corny. In addition, he worried that he had lost an ally. A crazy ally who was obviously much smarter and more in tune with daily happenings than anyone suspected.

"I guess I'd better go find my parents," Jae said. "If they somehow haven't heard already... news travels fast..." he sped off.

"Maybe the poor man's finally at peace," Meghan said. "Still, wacko. Why did he need to find *you* first," she asked her brother. "And what the heck did he mean? Hope or death?"

Colin had not realized she had heard Corny say it.

"I honestly have no clue. He really freaked me out there for a minute though. I thought he could see... you know ..."

"Did seem like that," Meghan agreed.

"It's okay, Colin," Catrina told him. "Whether for some reason he could or not, it does not matter now, does it?"

"No. You're right. It doesn't matter now."

The news of the sudden death of the caravans' resident crazy man did not take long to spread. Later in the evening, nearly all Svoda made an appearance at Corny's hastily prepared funeral, to pay their respects to this once respected and sane man.

Colin was surprised at how many people had known Corny before he had ended up a hermit who preferred to live in cramped, dark places.

The funeral also dampened the group's already dulled spirits. Because regardless of his last few years, Corny's life and death were just another grim reminder of the toll this life took on them all.

Meghan rushed off as soon as the funeral was completed.

Jae stayed by his parents' side, accepting condolences for Corny's passing. Most people just praised the Mochries for taking him in and caring for him. Colin heard comment after comment saying things like, "I don't know how you did it these last few years..." or "What patient people you must be..." and "You really made a difference in his life, gave him a reason to live."

For some reason, all of these comments bothered Colin.

"What's wrong?" asked Catrina, seeing the obvious frustration.

Colin could not express his thoughts clearly and just shook his head.

"What is *that*?" Catrina suddenly asked him, pointing.

Colin jerked his head to look where she pointed, just as an eight-legged shadow vanished behind some nearby bushes.

"Pajak! Juliska's pet," he told Catrina.

"Is it spying on you?" she asked.

Colin did not reply. Was it safe to? Was his every move being watched? Did they know about Catrina? Did they know that Corny had somehow helped him, even in his seemingly crazy state of mind?

"I need to get out of here!" Colin suddenly blurted. "I feel like I can't... breathe."

"Let's go then," Catrina insisted.

"Where to? It's not safe to leave the meadow."

"Maybe your book can help us with that."

"Actually... you're right!" he exclaimed. "If I can make you invisible, why not myself too!" He proceeded to use the same spell on himself as he did on Catrina and they rushed hand in hand out of the meadow. He was sure to add the *Abdo* before any spell, to keep the traces of magic hidden from anyone who might be tracking it.

"We could have just stayed," she said, after a short walk through the dense forest.

"I know. No one can see or hear us. I just needed to get away from there."

"Sad about Corny?"

"Sad. Confused. Torn. About Corny, about..." he paused, sitting on a fallen log. "Catrina, I need to know. Do you know who left you in the cave? Or were you telling Ivan the truth when you said you didn't know."

She sighed. "It was the truth, but I have my suspicions."

"Juliska Blackwell," he confirmed.

"Yes. But not just her, there were others, too. I don't think she acted alone."

"But why? Why would they do that to you? You're harmless!"

"Not everyone might agree with that Colin."

He stood and took her hand.

"You can trust me with anything," he told her. "If they think you're the Projector, I will prove them wrong!"

Catrina's eyes began to moisten.

"Oh, Colin. I..."

A branch snapped nearby. Instinctively, Colin grasped Catrina and started running. They stopped only once they had run so far, that they began to fear they might get lost. Colin wondered if maybe getting lost wouldn't actually be a good thing.

"It's pretty dark in here," noted Catrina.

"We'll be okay," assured Colin. "I'll find the way back."

A rustling in the tree above his head startled him.

"Bird!"

The mysterious bird human rested on a branch, in bird form. It nodded hello and then flew down.

"I guess I should stop being surprised when you pop in to visit," Colin said, feeling slightly more cheerful. Bird chirped his response in a manner that Colin somehow understood meant he was trying to tell him something.

"You could just transform," Colin suggested. To his and Catrina's surprise, Bird did transform, but at a distance and behind a tree.

"Sorry. I can't let you see me," he spoke. "But there's something I need to show you, and I can only see you two when I'm in bird form, as you have a cloaking spell on you that hides you from human eyes."

"I'd forgotten about the cloaking spell," said Colin. "It honestly didn't even dawn on me. So you can see us, in your bird form, but not your human form?"

"Yes. Correct."

Colin and Catrina had the same terrifying thought. Pajak was not human.

"We'll worry about that later," Colin whispered. "What do you need to show us, Bird?"

"Stay cloaked," he first warned. "No matter what, do not show yourselves."

The flapping of wings overhead indicated that Bird had transformed back into his flying form. He flapped and pointed his beak, motioning for them to follow.

They trudged carefully through the woods, following. They did not follow a path, so progress was at times slow. Eventually however, the forest began to lighten. Bird flew to a low tree branch, next to Colin's face. He pointed his beak toward the light, still chirping.

Catrina smiled.

"What?" questioned Colin.

"His chirping is musical. I'm starting to understand what he's saying," she said.

"How?" asked Colin.

Before she could answer, voices echoed into the forest.

"He is warning us again, to remain cloaked," whispered Catrina, "as we are not alone."

They crept cautiously ahead.

"Another meadow," Colin noted.

"Stripers," Catrina added. "What are they building?"

"I can't tell from here. Let's get a little closer," he said.

They crawled as close to the edge as they dared, being careful not to snap any branches or rustle any bushes. They might be invisible, but so could be the chameleon-like Stripers, and now that they knew the invisibility spell had limitations, they knew they should not take unnecessary chances.

Once in better view, Colin knew instantly what they were building.

"Pyres," he spoke ominously.

Bird landed on the ground next to them and nodded in agreement. A sinking feeling nearly made Colin become sick. What were they planning? This meadow was easily twice as wide as the meadow the Svoda camped in, and pyres dotted nearly the entire space. Colin tried to count but lost track after forty-three.

Even more suspicious, was that in the center of each pyre, shot up a single pole, with tethers clearly meant for tying up something or someone.

"I think we need to leave," Colin advised. "I don't know what this means, but we definitely need to warn the others!"

"I agree," Catrina said. "Something about this is very wrong."

Bird led the way and bade them farewell at the edge of the Svoda's meadow. Colin took off the cloaking spell that made him invisible. He stepped out from behind a tent and directly into Ivan Crane.

"Colin! Hello!" Ivan said, astonished at the sudden appearance. He also nodded cautiously at the emptiness next to Colin, assuming Catrina stood by his side.

"She says hi, but never mind that right now. I need your help! Is there somewhere we can *talk*?" he whispered.

Ivan's face turned serious and he motioned for them to follow. He stopped at the Mochrie tent, which was empty.

"Nowhere is truly safe, but this should suffice."

Colin undid the spell on Catrina so Ivan could see her.

"We left the meadow," Colin admitted.

"Why should it not surprise me that you're breaking the rules?" Ivan said dryly.

"Doesn't matter right now, Ivan. We came across the treasure hunters. They're up to something."

"Something very bad," Catrina stated.

Colin explained the field of pyres, and as he did so, Ivan's face turned at first concerned and then furious.

"There is definitely more going on than the Stripers are admitting," he agreed.

"The problem is, how do we warn everyone? We weren't supposed to leave the meadow... we shouldn't have seen anything... "

Ivan and Colin stared at each other for a long while.

"The Banon must be made aware. This is too important to hide," Ivan finally spoke.

"Wait!" Catrina said. "I think I have an idea."

Colin and Ivan listened as she explained.

"Will she go along with it?" asked Ivan, after Catrina had finished.

"She'll have to!" Colin said. "It's the only safe way." Colin made attempts to reach Meghan through his mind. She did not answer.

Ivan looked at Colin with a questioning face. Colin surrendered to the moment.

"Meghan and I, we can hear each others' thoughts," he admitted.

"That actually explains a lot," Ivan said.

Colin was not sure why he let Ivan in on their secret, but thus far, though temperamental, Ivan had never done anything to show he could not be trusted.

"She's not answering right now though," Colin said.

"She is training with the Banon," Ivan replied. I just left there when I happened upon you." He darted to the tent exit. "I will make an excuse to return and somehow tell Meghan to … read your mind, or however it works. This cannot wait. Lives could depend on this information."

Ivan dashed to return to Meghan.

Colin recast his spell on Catrina and departed the Mochries' tent, heading for Billie's. With each step he took, he kept a wary eye searching for Pajak. All he hoped was that this news of the pyres would be enough to sidetrack Juliska Blackwell, until he had a chance to deal with the spying spider that most likely, had seen Catrina.

After visiting with his parents, Sebastien Jendaya found himself standing at the front door of Amelia Cobb's office. The leader of the banished Svoda knew he had arrived.

"Come in," he heard her say.

He put on a smile and entered.

"Please, sit, Sebastien. Would you like anything to drink, or eat?" she asked, refilling a coffee mug for herself.

Sebastien patted his stomach. "I think my mother just fed me all of the meals I missed over the last few weeks, and the ones I will most likely miss over the coming weeks," he replied.

Amelia chuckled. "I really lucked out with you, Sebastien. When I planted you as a young boy, to befriend the Jacoby twins, I had no idea what an asset you would become to me."

Sebastien just nodded. *You neglected to tell me the part about how they would suffer...*

"And yet I feel like I have stolen your childhood," she admitted apologetically.

"Like you always say, we all have our part to play. And for mine, I will do whatever I can to help my friends."

"Yes. It at least gives me slight comfort that you became so close over the years."

And that is somehow supposed to make all of this okay? Sebastien reined in his thoughts. This was the wrong place to let his true feelings show.

"I've had contact," Sebastien informed her. "I got a *call* from Meghan. Her skills as a Firemancer are advancing."

"Splendid!" Amelia cried. "This is good news indeed. And we needed some, after what's been going on these last weeks."

"My dad told me about the Projector. Has any decision been made?"

"Debates are ongoing. The entire community has weighed in at this point, but everyone has a different view on the matter, as I'm sure you can imagine. But our goals remain the same. The only question is, if this Projector can get us there, or will keep us from succeeding."

"Frankly, I don't see how it's possible that a Projector could be of any use. I only know what I learned in school of course," Sebastien added.

"And many agree with you, my young friend. It is difficult to see how harnessing a Projector's power could help us return magic to its full glory. I fear the child is lost. If not by our hand, then another's."

"It's hard to imagine," he said, "having magic return. Do you think the world is really ready for it?"

"This is why we have worked so hard to get people in the right places, Sebastien. To be certain that when we heal the world, and return magic, that we can control the situation. We will be ready to teach and return this world to the glory it once was. Won't it be nice not to hide anymore?"

Sebastien thought about that question for a long minute before answering. He felt as though he had been hiding his entire life.

"That will be nice, yes."

His thoughts shifted to his new quest and the secrets he had discovered. Not having to hide, lie or betray *would* be very nice, but not for the reasons Amelia Cobb had stated. Sebastien did not know if returning magic was a good idea or not, but since the revelation that his friends were involved in Amelia's plans, and from the little information he had been able to squeeze from her or his parents, his gut told him his friends were in serious trouble.

What Sebastien did not understand is how their Uncle Arnon could have allowed all of this to happen... then again, it was likely that Arnon had no more idea than he did, as to what Amelia was planning. At least he hoped not. Thinking of Arnon Jacoby betraying the siblings was a devastating thought.

"Well, onto business," Amelia continued. "As Meghan is now *calling*, I think it best to wait until she contacts you again. From what my other informant has told me, she is not yet ready to know the truth, and therefore, what she will need to do. They feel the time is nearing, however."

Typical vague answer ... Sebastien wanted to kick himself. *You need to keep it together until you know what's really going on!*

"Until then, Sebastien, continue with your current mission."

"Very well," Sebastien replied. He could not get out of her office fast enough.

The one thing he was sure of: he was running out of time to help Meghan.

And what of Colin? Amelia never mentioned him in any specific manner, but he could feel that she was hiding something...

Sebastien wished now, more than ever, that he had come clean with the twins. He wished he had told them everything he knew about magic and who they were believed to be. He wished he had given them some warning about what was to come. He wished he had known they weren't even twins! Probably not even related!

All I can do is try and help them now ... and hope that I can...

Sebastien could not wait to leave home, again. He knew, however, that he needed to look pleased to be home and not in a hurry to leave... other than looking eager to get back to work.

Now that he knew Meghan's mother was alive, he wanted to disappear. To take what he knew and help his friends. He feared that what he knew was not enough. He could, at least, tell them they could go home whenever they wanted...tell them that their Uncle Arnon was ...

"You know you have to stay," he told himself as he approached home. "Meghan's mother is right. There is so much more at stake, and I can't mess this up!"

He took out the candle meant for Meghan.

His lives were colliding.

His job for Ameila Cobb.

His friendship with the twins.

His quest to save them.

His duty to his family and his fellow banished Svoda.

The job he had been trained for his entire life... to befriend, report, and eventually, to betray ...

##

Ivan poked his head into the Banon's tent. Jelen and Jenner did not question his return, seeing as Ivan visited a few times each day.

"Pantin Hollee," he said upon entering.

She perked up at seeing his face. "Back so soon," she joked.

"I had to pass back by and ran into Ms. Jacoby's brother. Told him I'd pass along a message."

"The Banon just departed, the meeting starts soon you know," she reminded. "Meghan's in her room," she pointed, while organizing a stack of papers.

"Thank you!" Ivan rapped at the entrance to Meghan's room.

"Come in," her voice called out. Meghan sat on the floor with Nona by her side, reading. Her face turned sour as she saw it was Ivan.

"Meghan, I have a message for you from your brother," he told her, loud enough for the Pantin to hear.

"From Colin?" she asked, standing.

"He asked me to pass along that he'd like to hear from you," he said with an edge of knowingness.

Her eyes narrowed and then grew large. She immediately opened up her thoughts and realized he had been trying desperately to reach her.

"Colin, I'm sorry," she sent him. "I was so focused on my studies I didn't hear you." She added hotly, "Why on earth did you tell Ivan about our telepathy?"

"Sorry, Sis. Didn't have a choice." Colin opened up his mind and showed her what he had seen in the Striper's meadow.

"What do you think they're doing?" she asked him, as horrified about the scene as the others.

"We don't know. But Ivan is right, Juliska needs to know." Colin then sent her Catrina's idea.

"Oh, I agree, Col. I don't see any other safe way either."

Meghan refocused on Ivan, still waiting in her room. "C'mon," she motioned, stepping into the front room. The Pantin was just about to leave, but stopped when she saw Ivan and Meghan.

"Thank you for passing along my brother's message, Ivan," Meghan said. "Please tell him I will visit as soon as I can."

Ivan stepped to the stove. "Fire's nearly out. It's rather chilly don't you think?" Ivan opened up the stove, adding a log, without waiting for an answer.

"Isn't he just sweet," the Pantin aimed toward Meghan, clearly seeing concern from Ivan that was not truly there.

Ivan just needed to get a fire in front of Meghan's eyes. The instant he opened the door Meghan fell into a vision, except this time, she was faking.

"Wait!" she shouted at the Pantin. "I need to see Banon Blackwell, now!" Meghan pretended to falter and Ivan steadied her. "Please, Hollee," Meghan pleaded. "I think what I've just seen might prove dangerous for everyone here."

The Pantin did not question and rushed off.

Ivan let go of Meghan.

"Not bad, huh."

"I have never questioned your acting ability," he retorted.

"Whatever," she replied.

"It shows promise, at least, that when you saw the fire you didn't have an *actual* vision," he taunted.

"Especially seeing as you're so near," she threw back at him.

For once, Ivan did not reply and remained silent until Juliska returned. Then, Meghan told her what she had seen.

"A field of pyres, created by the Stripers?" She sat down, aghast at the thought. She unexpectedly took hold of Meghan's hand.

"Thank you, Meghan. I knew having you here would not be a mistake. This could be the very clue we so desperately needed." She arose to depart.

"Back to the meeting?" asked the Pantin.

"Yes. We must decide what to do about this. I fear that once again, time is not on our side, my dear Hollee."

Ivan followed, leaving Meghan alone. She reopened her mind to Colin.

"It's done. She knows. They're meeting about it right now." She sensed her brother's relief.

"Thanks, Sis. Sorry to make you lie."

"Ah. What's new?" she retorted. "Why did you leave the meadow?" she then questioned.

"Just needed some space," he said honestly. "Plus, I wanted to talk to Catrina. We're back at Billie's now."

"Oh. Did you find out anything new about Catrina?"

"Only things you're not going to like to hear, Sis."

She knew he meant that Juliska was somehow involved.

"Colin, Juliska couldn't have had anything to do with abandoning Catrina in that cave," she defended.

"Maybe you're right," he said. "But Catrina seems to think that maybe she did."

"And you believe her, a near stranger, more than your own sister, who lives with Juliska Blackwell?" Meghan's temper began to flare.

"Meghan," he said in a manner that indicated he had something important to tell her. "I think Catrina might be the Projector..." Even though he spoke it through his thoughts, his inner voice was low and uncertain.

Meghan, in shock by what Colin told her, could not reply. Her mind was blank as he searched for some response.

"I think Juliska, and possibly others, believe it at least," he added when she did not reply. "But I don't. I know she's not."

"Colin, I don't completely understand this whole Projector thing, but I know enough to realize it is NOT a good thing! What if it is her, Colin? That means she's dangerous! I do get weird vibes when I'm around her," she let slip out.

"What do you mean? Weird vibes?" he shot back.

"Colin. I'm sorry. I know you like her, but if I'm completely honest, something about her just doesn't feel right... and if Juliska thinks..."

She felt Colin's block go back in its place and lost her connection to him. She attempted repeatedly to reconnect, but he ignored her.

"Crap!" she shouted to no one. She wanted to use much stronger words. "Leave it to my brother to fall in love with the Projector. They'll kill her!"

Then, as she thought about it, her worries increased even more.

"If he tries to save her... they'll kill him too! And I don't even want to think about what Catrina might do to him..."

She hastened out of the tent, unsure of what to do. Just then, the ground began to shake. Another quake. She grabbed onto a tent pole, hoping to stay upright. She heard a terrible swooshing and then a crash nearby, followed by a scream.

The shaking stopped. Once steady on her feet, she turned toward the crash. A tree had fallen at the edge of the meadow onto a tent.

She raced over, as did others. Her fear: someone was inside stuck under the tree, or worse, killed by it. After a quick search, a teenage girl was discovered passed out, underneath a branch, but alive.

Doctor Stamm arrived just a minute later to examine the girl, and to Meghan's surprise, so did Ivan. He looked gravely concerned over the girl's condition.

Meghan recognized the girl, from school in Grimble. If she remembered correctly, the girl's name was Maria and she was sixteen years old.

Mostly, Meghan recalled thinking that the girl was pretty, but also shy. Whenever Meghan had seen the girl, she was alone.

"I need to get her back to my tent," Dr. Stamm said. "She looks to be okay at first glance, but I need to do a more thorough examination. It does look as if the branch hit her head," he added, concernedly.

Meghan was surprised again, when Ivan stepped in and picked up the girl, carrying her away.

"I wonder..." *Does he like her? Is it possible that I've discovered a secret about the mysterious Ivan Crane?* She secretly delighted in the idea.

Those that remained behind helped to push the tree off the tent and back to the edge of the meadow. Then, they headed to see if help was needed elsewhere.

Meghan decided to join them, temporarily sidetracked by her worries from just minutes before.

##

Colin was furious. He should have never admitted his fears about Catrina. Especially not to his sister, as she was so close to Juliska Blackwell. But if not Meghan, then who? Was there anyone he could trust? Balloch Flummer's warning *not to*

163

trust anyone came to mind, yet again. Surely, he could trust his own sister.

The more he thought about what he had done the angrier he became. His hands trembled and his heart pounded in his chest. He wanted to hit something. Hard.

"What happened?" Catrina begged.

"I will never let anyone hurt you!" he spouted without explanation.

"Hurt me?" she repeated. "What did Meghan tell you?"

Underneath them, the ground started to quiver.

Colin did not answer as in the next moment he fell backwards, the ground shaking violently now.

"Colin! What did she say?" demanded Catrina.

Colin looked up at her, his face contorted with confusion. "Are you causing this?" he asked her.

"What? The quake?" she said, falling to his side. "Why would you think that?"

Just one look into her eyes and any fear Colin felt vanished. How could this small, silver-haired girl be dangerous? He nearly laughed at the thought.

The ground began to quiet again.

"I'm sorry," Colin whispered. "I am ..." he did not want to admit how he felt. "I'm afraid, Catrina. I'm really afraid."

He was afraid that if Catrina knew how frightened he was, she would not wish to stay with him. That she would think he was weak and unable to protect her. But his greatest fear: *She is the one the Stripers are searching for... and how can I possibly protect her if she is the Projector? I'm just a boy that happens to be good at magic...*

"Colin," she whispered back. "You're not the only one that's afraid." She nestled into his side. "Promise me you won't ever leave me," she muttered under her breath. "I know we hardly know each other, and people would say we're just young and naive, but ... I love you, Colin Jacoby. I'm so sure of it I'd bet my life on it this very moment! No matter what happens, I will never leave you."

Colin sat up. Spending a lifetime with Catrina would never be enough time. Maybe she was a stranger, but like Catrina, he knew what he wanted, and he wanted to be with her. He got to his feet, helping her up off the ground.

He kissed her and wiped away the tears now streaming down her face.

"I won't let you live in fear. I will do whatever it takes to keep you safe!" He paused, disbelieving what he was about to say. "Because I know that I love you too, Catrina Flummer. I knew it the first moment I saw you, and nothing will ever changer that."

They sat down on the bed, staring at each other, frightened, and yet knowing that somehow, whatever happened, they would at least always be together.

##

Meghan wandered through the meadow, assisting in clean up after the quake. Her attempts to contact Colin were futile.

"Hey, stranger," she heard someone shout.

"Hey Jae," she replied rather somberly, upon seeing him.

"Looks like they've got all of us non-Initiated doing all the cleaning," he joked.

"I need a distraction anyway," she muttered, her gaze sweeping to the other side of the meadow, toward the meeting tent. "I wonder if they've decided anything yet?"

"Decided what?" Jae asked her.

Meghan explained to Jae what Bird had shown Colin and Catrina in the Stripers' meadow.

"A field of pyres..." he shuddered at the thought. "Got my curiosity. I wonder what Banon Blackwell's going to do about it?"

"That's what I've been waiting to find out," Meghan replied. "We've been cleaning up after the quake for over two hours. I was hoping they'd have finished by now."

"I may have never been to an SLC meeting, but one thing I've learned... they rarely decide on anything quickly."

They moved into the cantina, where everything was still a mess from the quake. Pots and pans were lying on the ground, tables and chairs were knocked over, and utensils were strewn across the ground. Just then, a couple of pots fell, clanging together, crashing to the ground.

Jae jumped, startled. His eyes darted back and forth, as if searching for some unknown assailant.

Jae's a little jumpier than normal. "Everything okay?" Meghan asked him.

"Huh? Oh, yeah, fine." He returned to cleaning up the cantina.

"I know you've been living this lifestyle a lot longer than I have, Jae, but to be honest, I still don't know how. Sometimes, I can't help but think about how simple it would be, to just be back in Cobbscott... back before I knew anything about magic or Firemancy."

Jae stopped cleaning.

"It seems so long ago now, doesn't it? That I got stuck in Cobbscott."

"Seems like ancient history!"

"Sometimes, Meghan, I miss that time. A lot. Being stuck in Cobbscott ... I just... want to be back there."

Meghan waited for him to speak, eager that he might actually open up to her.

Jae sighed. He looked down at the ground and then directly at Meghan. She could tell he was desperate to say something, but literally looked as though he could not speak the words.

"It's too late," he muttered. "Too late. Can't go back, now."

"What do you mean Jae?" she asked, surprised at the sudden turn in their conversation.

She reached for his arm.

"Don't touch me!" he exhaled, backing up. "You should just leave me alone! I wish... I wish I'd never gotten left behind in Cobbscott... because I wouldn't have ... I've really made a mess of things, Meghan." Jae's face looked hopeless as he suddenly ran away.

Meghan stomped on the ground. *How much can one person take!* She wanted to locate Ivan and demand, on the spot, that he tell her everything he knew about Jae Mochrie. She needed to solve *something*. Not everything could just be question after question and new problem after new problem. At some point, there had to be an answer that did not lead to more questions, or bigger problems!

In the distance, people started to leave the meeting tent. *Meeting must be over.* Instinct told her she should return to Juliska's tent.

It was Ivan, not Juliska that greeted her.

"Just the person I wanted to see!" she told him, clearly irritated.

"What's got you all worked up?"

She set her jaw and stood with her hands on her hips. "You know what, Ivan Crane? You are the most loathsome person I know!"

"I'm going to guess that this has nothing to do with the meeting?"

"No, Ivan. It doesn't. And you know what I am 'all worked up' about!"

"Ah," he stated. "Always comes back to this, doesn't it? We have an agreement, Meghan," he leaned in, reminding her.

"How could I forget, Ivan?" she angrily whispered back. "Jae just completely freaked out on me. Why?" she demanded.

He stared at her until finally deciding to reply.

"Whatever you're thinking is wrong with him, you're not right. Just let it go for now, Meghan."

"Why? Until when? It's too late to help him?"

He started to walk away.

"Don't just walk away, Ivan. Tell me!"

She gasped as he spun around and grabbed her unkindly, yanking her body into her room inside Juliska's tent.

"Just leave it alone, Meghan. What's happening to Jae is far worse than anything you could imagine or have seen in your visions!" he spat out viciously.

Meghan held her breath.

"It's NOT something you're ready to see! Or accept."

Ivan let go of her and turned away. Before leaving the tent, he lowered his head and sighed.

"I don't want you to bring it up again. I know you just want to help your friend. But you can't. No one can, Meghan," his voice cracked. "I really am sorry, but this is a reality you simply have to accept."

He left the tent, letting the canvas door slide down behind him.

Meghan slumped to the ground, tears falling freely down her face. She got to her knees and crawled to her bed, unable to find the strength to climb onto it.

"I just want to go home," she cried, crumpling into a ball.

Nona found her way in moments later and lay next to her.

"I just want to go back to being a nobody," she told her loyal pet.

Nona remained silent and allowed Meghan to sob, realizing nothing she said or did would give her any solace.

After awhile, Meghan stopped crying and just lay on the ground, all of her thoughts, fears and questions looping in circles in her mind.

"There is no going back, is there Nona?" she muttered.

"You know the answer, Meghan."

"Well, at least there's one thing I can control!" she raved, jumping off the ground and racing out of the tent.

The last thought Nona heard in Meghan's mind was something to do with Catrina being a Projector and her brother being in danger...

##

Colin arrived at Billie's later that evening. He had left Catrina in his room while he grabbed them both dinner. He froze just outside after hearing an unwelcome voice.

"Garner," he frowned.

"So they've sent out another hunting party?" Billie was saying.

"Yes. The Banon feels it necessary to make it look like a hunting party, for the sake of the

Stripers, but they'll be looking into the pyres. They should report back before nightfall."

"Which isn't too long from now, my brother."

"I am sorry I have not visited sooner," Garner apologized. "Things are... complicated."

"You don't have to tell me. Right mess we got going!"

"Maybe better now that the boy is staying with you," Garner said.

"Yes, better I suppose. Better to be away from the Mochrie boy."

"Jae?" muttered Colin. What did they mean?

"Is there no hope for him?" continued Billie, her voice barely audible.

"He made the choice, Billie. You know I cannot interfere."

"Right complicated mess," she sighed. "And the boy, Colin, he's been acting rather oddly," Billie admitted.

Colin's eyes widened. He had not been careful enough. And now, Garner Sadorus was too close to finding out about Catrina. He took a few steps back and then noisily made his way to the tent's entrance. He needed to end this conversation.

##

Meghan Jacoby ignored the pleas from Nona, begging her to rethink what she was about to do.

"Sorry, Nona," she said, seeing Juliska heading toward the tent.

Meghan backed inside, her heart racing as she neared.

"I have to do this. It's for his own good. I have always looked out for Colin. I know what's best!"

Juliska entered the tent looking worn. "Megan..."

"There is something I must tell you," Meghan exclaimed. "It cannot wait and I think it best we talk in *your* room."

Meghan's intimation peaked Juliska's curiosity instantly.

"Very well." Juliska motioned for Meghan to follow her in. "Have you had another vision?"

"No vision. But I haven't been completely honest with you about something and now, because of that, I fear for my brother's life."

Meghan took a deep breath and began, before she could lose her nerve.

"I think I know who the Projector is, and where you can find her!"

Juliska's face turned at first white, and then red with anger.

"What exactly do you mean, Meghan?"

"Remember when my brother followed Ivan and myself into Eidolon's Valley? While he was there, he found a girl."

Juliska nearly lost her balance. "A girl?" she stammered. "And what happened to said girl?" her voice rose an octave while asking.

Meghan gulped hard. "He brought her with us and cast some sort of spell that cloaked her, made her invisible to anyone else. We didn't know he'd done it," she lied, for Ivan's sake, knowing it would be bad for him if Juliska thought *he* had lied, too. Meghan swallowed and stated her case.

"I think she's the Projector the Stripers are looking for. I should have told you sooner, I'm sorry... I think she is infecting him," she added maliciously.

The normally composed Juliska Blackwell crumpled. The veins on her face turned blue against her pale skin. The longer Juliska held in her emotion, the veins turned flame red, like bright tattoos lining her skin.

"There are things you obviously cannot understand, Meghan," Juliska spoke fervently. "But I am glad you have told me this. Your brother is in serious danger." She added, "Catrina Flummer was left in that valley for a reason!"

"What?" Meghan asked, thinking she had not heard correctly.

"I should have taken care of the job myself!" Juliska shouted as she angrily stormed out of the room.

Meghan lost her breath, falling to her knees. *What just happened?*

"She knew," muttered Meghan. *Juliska knew that Catrina was left in the cave... Catrina was right...* "This doesn't matter," Meghan spoke, mostly to comfort herself. "Catrina is still dangerous, and Juliska knew this, too."

"Jelen! Jenner!" Meghan heard Juliska shout just outside her room. "There is an intruder in our camp. I want you to locate Colin Jacoby and bring him in, immediately!"

They departed at once to begin their search.

Meghan mustered up enough strength to leave Juliska's room.

Pantin Hollee arrived a second later.

"Sound the alarm, Hollee. I want Colin Jacoby found, now!"

Hollee darted her eyes between Juliska and Meghan but did not question. Meghan stared blankly at the tent wall.

"I am sorry Meghan," Juliska spoke heartlessly. "But this is something that cannot go unpunished. But be comforted, that if we locate Catrina Flummer, your brother will at least live."

175

Juliska whispered, so Meghan could not hear, to Pajak, as he crawled out of her hair and onto her shoulder. "I should have listened to you, my pet. You told me he was talking to a girl you did not recognize..." She stormed off to join the search.

Meghan once again crumpled to the ground, and once again, Ivan Crane arrived just in time to pick her back up.

"I... I told Juliska about Catrina," she stuttered. "Colin told me he thinks she's the Projector..."

"Um. What?" he responded, so shocked that he nearly dropped her.

"I thought it was the right thing ... Oh God! Ivan ..."

"Can you reach him, through your mind?" he asked. "Maybe you shouldn't..." he was obviously as torn about this situation as Meghan.

Meghan tried to reach him, but Colin ignored her attempts.

"I think he's at Billie's. Everyone knows that's where he's staying. They'll go right there."

"Not if I get there first!" Nona shouted. "Ivan, open the stove door."

He did so at once, clearly making the choice to help Colin and Catrina. Why? Meghan didn't know and didn't care. Nona bounded into the flame, dissolving at once. The closest open flame

176

was three tents away from Billie's. As the Catawitch popped out of the flame, her legs were already running before they hit the ground.

Nona heard Meghan's thoughts as she ran.

I can't believe what I just did... I'm supposed to protect him... maybe I am protecting him... but he loves her... Colin will never forgive me for this... he shouldn't ever forgive me for this...

Nona ran as fast as she could toward Billie's, darting between unaware people, nearly tripping one man as she jumped through his legs.

"Oh please let me get there first!" she pleaded.

Chapter Six

Colin Jacoby entered Billie's tent.

The look on Garner's face gave away nothing about what he had meant about him not being around Jae Mochrie, or thankfully, that he knew anything about Catrina.

Before Colin could greet either Billie or Garner, a bell started clanging, sounding an alarm throughout the meadow.

Billie and Garner looked at each other, concerned. As they opened the tent door to see what the alarm was for, Nona came bounding in, screeching to a halt.

"Colin! They know about Catrina! They're coming for you!"

Colin dropped his tray of food.

The room started spinning.

He heard Catrina gasp.

He allowed his sisters' thoughts to flood his, realizing that it was *she* that had betrayed them.

Anger instantly flowed through his veins. *How could you? How could you do this?* His thoughts begged her to answer.

He turned his mind off to Meghan's river of apologies and raced into his room. There was nothing Meghan could say that would make up for this betrayal.

He needed to get Catrina to safety.

Garner and Billie followed him.

"Catrina?" Garner questioned. "Catrina Flummer?"

"Yes," Colin answered weakly, wondering how he had guessed.

Billie's hand went up to her mouth, covering it.

"Oh thank God!" Garner said. "We feared she was lost!"

"Huh?" Colin shook his head. Was nothing in this place as it appeared? Was anyone telling him the truth? *No wonder Balloch said to trust no one... I can't even trust my own sister...*

"Where is she?" Billie demanded.

Colin feared he had no choice but show her. He felt Catrina's hand close around his own and he lifted the spell. She materialized before them. Garner and Billie looked relieved, and just as quickly, frightened.

"You must leave," Garner advised.

"And go where?" Colin asked, still confused by Garner's assistance.

"There's no time!" reminded Nona.

"I will stall them as long as I can," Garner said, nodding at his sister.

"Follow me," ordered Billie.

Garner grasped Colin's shirt, stopping him.

"Protect this girl with your life! You have no idea how important she is!"

Billie ran out of the back of tent, shouting for Colin and Catrina to keep up. She kept to the back of the tents and out of sight, stopping four tents over.

Billie darted inside, followed by Colin and Catrina. They startled a woman, putting on shoes to head out of her tent.

"Billie!" spoke the startled voice of Sidra Flummer.

Noah Flummer, her son, came running out of a room at the back, shouting.

"What is it, Mother?" he stopped when he saw Billie Sadorus, Colin Jacoby and a girl he did not recognize.

Recognition hit them both just a mere second later.

"You're alive," Sidra muttered, running forward and grasping Catrina in her arms.

Catrina sobbed as Sidra held her close.

"Noah, Sidra, I'm sorry, there's little time to explain. This alarm is because our young Colin Jacoby has been hiding Catrina here in the camp since we arrived. I don't know the story. But Juliska's coming for them."

"They need to leave," Noah said as urgently as Garner had just minutes before.

"How will we get them out of here?" asked Sidra. "And where will they go?"

"Into the forest," said Noah, already packing a bag. He threw in what little food was in the tent and thrust the bag into Colin's hands.

"How?" Sidra asked Colin. "How did you..."

"It was your husband, Mam. Balloch... after he died, he came to me, told me where she was. I went into Eidolon's Valley and found her. I'm sorry I never told you. It's just that Balloch told me not to trust anyone. I should have realized I could trust her family."

He suddenly felt guilty for not seeking out their help before. Then again, his own sister had betrayed him... he buried his anger. He did not have time for it now.

"Don't apologize, Colin," Noah insisted. "What you did was more than brave. We'll never be able to thank you for saving her."

A voice shouted nearby.

"He's not there. Search every tent until you find him."

"We'll give you as much time as we can," Noah said.

"Where do we go after we're in the forest?" Colin asked, heading toward the back of the tent.

Noah lifted the bottom of the tent so he and Catrina could sneak through. No one knew what to tell him, and there was no time left to figure out any sort of plan. Footsteps approached the Flummer's tent.

Sidra grabbed Catrina, hugged her and then pushed her to Colin.

"Run. Run as fast as you can," she shouted as they dipped underneath the canvas and crawled into the woods.

Once in the woods Colin attempted to recast his spell, to hide them both, but it failed. His nerves had gotten the better of him. He could not make it work. Then he froze.

"The Magicante. I left it!"

"We can't go back, Colin," Catrina said, shakily.

She was right, but he felt useless without the book.

"There they are," a voice shouted, seeing them at the wood's edge.

Colin grasped Catrina and ran. He did not know where they were going. He didn't know how he was going to save her.

Whoever was chasing them was catching up.

183

Colin and Catrina were no match in a race on foot.

A voice ordered them to stop but they kept running, darting under branches and over fallen logs. The voice shouted again and Colin recognized it as either Jelen or Jenner, Juliska Blackwell's personal bodyguards.

"We're not going to make it," he said, fearful.

But they kept running.

The footsteps of Jelen and Jenner jutting at their ankles.

Catrina lost her grip and fell. Colin slid to a stop.

The two men caught up easily.

"Stay where you are!" Jelen ordered heavily.

"You are both under arrest!" Jenner added fiercely.

Colin jumped to his feet and helped Catrina stand. She wrapped her arms around his neck, afraid to look at the two men.

The guards stepped closer, and then stepped back, gaping at something behind Colin and Catrina. Colin did not know if he wanted to look, but did. A light began to emanate from a hollowed out tree and a face Colin thought he would never see again popped out from the shadows.

"I see I arrived in time," a grizzled voice spoke. "Come with me!"

He stepped back into the light.

Colin and Catrina took one look at Jelen and Jenner and knew they had no choice. Behind the men, the entire Svoda caravan approached. It was impossible for them not to see the two escapees, standing in front of the bright light, surrounded by the darkness of the forest.

"Who is that girl?" a voice asked.

Similar murmurings spread throughout the crowd.

No one, it seemed, understood what was happening.

"Stop them!" Juliska Blackwell shouted upon arrival, realizing they were about to escape.

Her bodyguards cautiously approached.

Meghan raced forward. "Colin, please, don't do this!" she pleaded. "Just let him go," she aimed at Catrina.

Meghan's body shockingly flew backwards through the air, landing with a soft thud on the thick forest floor. She felt some new force blocking her from Colin's mind. She tried to penetrate it, but it was stronger than anything she had ever felt before.

Colin entered her mind, one final time. His voice was venomous as he spoke.

"I won't *ever* forgive you for this, Sister."

Then, the connection she had known and felt her entire life, vanished.

It tore at her very fiber, crushing any hope she had left. This Colin Jacoby was not the Colin Jacoby she knew. Something in him changed, like a switch that flipped, turning him into something else.

Meghan cursed the day her brother discovered this girl, Catrina Flummer.

Jelen and Jenner bounded toward Colin and Catrina, who in turn, jumped into the light, which dissolved, leaving behind nothing but an empty, hollowed out tree.

A look of fury crossed Juliska's face and her veins, still flame red in color, looked as though they were popping out of her skin.

The entire Svoda caravan now stood in the forest.

Billie stood close by her brother and his wife, Ravanna. The Sadorus' nodded politely as the Flummer's walked passed them, acting as if nothing out of the ordinary had happened at all. They pretended to be ignorant of the fact that the girl standing next to Colin Jacoby was a relative. She was in another group after all… how would they know what she looked like?

Juliska shouted for the Viancourt members and Balaton to follow her. A heated, but private conversation began, not too far away.

While they held their meeting, the people started asking more questions. Many stares and glares shot toward Meghan and she backed up, trying to hide in the darkness. She did not know what to say or what was about to happen. It felt like her first day with the Svoda all over again.

She reached out in her mind for Colin but he was not there.

She felt empty. Alone.

Ivan suddenly appeared at her side.

"What's done is done," he whispered, actually sounding compassionate. "You did what you thought was right. Sometimes," he paused. "Sometimes, Meghan, what's right is not what's easy."

Meghan only half heard him. She felt as though she were about to faint. She wished she could somehow discover a way to go back in time and stop herself from telling Juliska about Catrina. At the same time, as happy as she was about Colin getting away, she feared for his life. Catrina was still dangerous.

"I might have been wrong," Ivan told her. "You might be ready to hear what I have to say about Jae, after all."

Meghan jerked her head to look at him, her face cold and emotionless.

He walked away.

This moment was not the right moment.

Meghan could not form words. She could barely stand. Up ahead, she heard a voice calling out to the group.

"Look! Look here!" it shouted.

The caravan began a mass movement toward a clearing, not too far away. Another meadow, Meghan noticed. As soon as it came into view, she froze.

"The meadow with the pyres," someone whispered. Jae Mochrie had said it.

She had not even noticed him step up next to her. He grasped her arm, gently.

"Ivan told me what happened," his eyes screamed that he understood how she felt. "I know this won't make you feel any better right now, but we all do things we wish we could take back. You can't change what happened..." he let go and headed, with the rest of the group, toward the edge of the meadow.

The setting darkness unraveled a horrifying scene.

The pyres were no longer empty.

The caravan stood at the edge of the meadow, looking in stunned abhorrence at the pyres, which now imprisoned the missing Svoda they had been searching for since their arrival. Gagged men, women and children had been bound to the pyres.

They appeared to be unconscious.

Fearful gasps and cries echoed into the meadow, as bodies of the chameleon-like Stripers starting materializing around the caravan, encircling them.

Juliska ordered silence with a single wave of her hand.

The leader of the Stripers, KarNavan, spoke.

"I will get right to the point. You are surrounded, and don't even think about using magic…" He pointed to the pyres. "These unlucky people are about to pay the ultimate price, unless you hand over what we seek."

"This is low, even for Stripers, KarNavan," the Banon replied. "Our magic may be weakened, but we still have enough to wage battle, if you force it upon us!"

"Actually, I think you'll find you are wrong," the Striper leader said. "Go ahead. Someone try to use magic."

Garner Sadorus stepped forward and attempted a simple spell. Nothing happened. The crowd gasped in horror. They truly were helpless.

"If this is about the Projector…" Juliska was cut off.

"Ah, yes. You see, we have tracked the child's magic, and the child *is* here! Alas, though, this is not the only job we are here to do," he admitted. "We look for another child, too. Or more to the point, something this child possesses." His words held no compassion.

The surrounded caravan huddled together. Parents held their children close and murmurs spread quickly but quietly.

KarNavan continued his speech.

"We seek a book! An ancient book. One currently owned by a boy named Colin Jacoby."

Meghan's head jerked up. The Magicante. As far as she knew, it was still at Billie's. She did not think Colin had taken it. Ivan, standing close by Juliska, glanced back at her, as if to ask if she knew where it was.

She shrugged, telling him she was not sure. All she did know was that she could not let Colin down, again. She would not allow these people to take it.

"How is it, that you are able to weaken our magic?" Juliska asked KarNavan. "You owe us at least, an answer to this question. We are, after all, descended from the same magical bloodlines."

"Same magical lines, eh? Interesting theory, Gypsy Queen." He winked at Juliska Blackwell. His voice insinuated some hidden meaning behind the words he spoke. "But why not, seeing as we are on the winning side."

He jumped onto a nearby pyre, grasping the pole.

The body bound to it stirred, slightly.

"We were hired," KarNavan explained, "to come here and collect two things: the Projector and a book. To insure success in our mission, we were given a most powerful and intriguing weapon."

He reached into his pocket, as if to take out something, but when he pulled his hand back out, it was empty. He waved around his empty palm.

"Did you really think we'd just tell you?" he toyed with Juliska.

"You can't blame a Queen for trying," she answered sourly.

"I will tell you this... if you give us what we want, we will permit you to leave, unharmed. Within hours, your magic will renew itself." He jumped down from the pyre. "However, if you do not heed our demands, you will each be stripped of your powers, completely, and you will watch each of your friends and loved ones burn!"

Voices began shouting at the Stripers.

"Who is this child you seek?"

"Do you know which child it is?"

It seemed as though the caravan was ready to surrender the child, rather than see everyone they loved suffer a painful fate.

Juliska, once again, silenced her people.

"Do you really think that we would just hand this child over to you freely? There have been no signs of a Projector in our camp."

Meghan knew this was not true. However, she also knew that the child in question was gone.

"Regardless," continued Juliska, "if the child was found and belonged to one of our own, we would end the life swiftly, before harm could be done. I would *never* turn it over to the likes of you. There's a difference between killing because you must, and showing *no* mercy or compassion."

KarNavan smiled.

"Now we get to it, don't we? You travelers. You think you're special, don't you? And yet, you have no idea what is truly happening in the magical world. You have not heard the rumblings. There is a war coming... a war to change the course of our world. And I, for one, will not be left behind when it's over."

"Who hired you?" Juliska demanded to know.

"You know already," he answered scathingly. "Who would have the capabilities to strip power from the powerful?"

"Grosvenor," Garner muttered.

KarNavan's savage eyes agreed with the answer.

Ivan worked his way back to Meghan. Jae stood to her other side. Ivan whispered as close to her ear as he could, without making it apparent that he was talking.

"Catrina," was all he said.

"Juliska must have hid her in the cave, thinking it was a better fate to sleep, rather than kill her," Jae muttered.

Ivan nodded in agreement.

Meghan stood motionless. Was it good or bad that Colin and Catrina were gone? Had she endangered him even more, by forcing him to flee to some unknown place, with a ticking time bomb at his side? A time bomb he clearly loved. Or could this whole ordeal be over and everyone's lives spared, if Catrina had been turned over now?

She sighed. Colin would never forgive her either way.

"There has to be a solution to all of this," she mumbled.

Just then, a Striper came running out of the forest and into the meadow.

"KarNavan! Wait!" a woman spoke.

"What do you have to report?"

"Our tracking system says the Projector is gone! Not here anymore."

"Definitely Catrina," Meghan heard Ivan say.

"What do you mean?" KarNavan demanded.

"The Projector's magic has disappeared. Plus, we searched their tents for the book. No sign of it!"

No sign of it... Meghan wondered what had happened to the book.

"It seems your presence here is no longer required," Juliska made claim. "The Projector and this book you're looking for have vanished."

"Ah, but it *was* here," KarNavan spoke tauntingly. "Didn't you feel the quakes? It's one of the first signs of uncontrolled magic."

The caravan looked inquisitively at each other. They had thought the quakes were just something that happened in this place.

"I believe the child you are searching for left this place, not many minutes ago, in fact," Juliska revealed to the Stripers. "And your tracking system now proves that. So let us go in peace, now."

"And what of the book?" the leader reminded. "I still want the book! One of you is hiding it!" KarNavan looked as though his patience was about to break. He picked up a torch and stormed back to the pyre he had just jumped down from, minutes before, threatening to light the kindling.

It became apparent that the person tied to the pyre was not completely unconscious, just greatly weakened, as the woman's eyes filled with fright, but she could barely move. She lifted her head, her eyes pleading for help.

Billie Sadorus rushed to the front of the group, shouting. "Maura!" she screamed. "Let her go!" Billie pleaded. "Put me in her place, please, I beg you!"

Tears fell down the face of the woman on the pyre named Maura when she saw Billie.

Garner rushed forward and tried to control Billie.

Meghan came out of her mournful stupor, as it dawned on her that she did not feel weakened. Perhaps the weapon the Stripers were using did not did not work on a Firemancer's powers. Then, wouldn't Juliska have used hers?

"Maybe she doesn't realize," Meghan muttered, envisioning what she must do.

She focused on the torch KarNavan held in his hand, as he waved it threateningly over the pyre. The flames nearly swiped Maura's body and she cried out in angst.

It took every bit of strength for Garner to hold back Billie. She kicked and beat on him, demanding he let her go.

Meghan lifted her own hand, held her palm open, and then shut it like a fist. The fire on KarNavan's torch flickered and dissolved as if suffocated.

Meghan did this repeatedly, thrusting the meadow into darkness.

An eerie smile appeared on KarNavan's face.

"Who is using magic?" he asked, stalking about, searching for the culprit.

A loud boom and a fiery explosion set off at the edge of the meadow, stealing everyone's attention. A block of trees burned, but not close enough to accidentally light any of the pyres.

"Good job, Meghan!" said Jae, impressed.

"That wasn't me," she replied, just as shocked as everyone else.

Ivan, Jae and Meghan searched the edge of the woods for any sign of their hidden savior, but saw nothing.

The Stripers began to back off from the caravan.

Juliska Blackwell moved forward, stepping in front of KarNavan.

"We may not be able to use magic, but..." she finished her statement by punching him in the face.

She still doesn't know she can use Firemancy... Meghan did not see any safe way to tell her.

KarNavan rubbed his jaw, clearly impressed by Juliska's blow.

"Stop this madness!" she demanded. "We obviously don't have what you're looking for. What good will come from hurting innocent people?"

"I always have liked your style," he muttered under his breath.

She glared at him, speaking low, so that only he could hear.

"I don't know what's really behind all of this, but it ends, now. None of this is part of the plan, KarNavan."

"Well maybe plans have changed," he shot back under his breath.

He backed away from her, ignoring her questioning gaze.

"What we seek is no longer here," he told his followers, declaring it was time for them to depart.

The Stripers retreated. Their bodies dissolving and melting into their backgrounds, but it took many long minutes before the sound of breaking branches and debris breaking under footsteps dissipated, leaving the Svoda, at last, alone and safe.

They then earnestly set in to releasing their fellow comrades.

Reunions would have to wait however, as most of the imprisoned people were sick and weak, barely able to comprehend what had occurred.

Billie ran to the woman named Maura, and with Garner's assistance, freed her from her bonds. The woman flung her arms weakly around Billie, sobbing.

"I thought I was going to lose you forever," Billie told the woman.

Juliska swept through the meadow, shouting orders.

In the next few hours' chaos, no one noticed Meghan, Jae and Ivan walking to the opposite edge of the meadow. They searched the area surrounding the exploded trees, but found no clues to indicate how the explosion had occurred.

"Whatever or whomever it was," said Ivan, "it scared away the Stripers."

"We can at least be thankful for that," added Jae, turning to head back into the meadow. Meghan stopped him by blurting out what they had all really wanted to say.

"So we all agree that the Projector is Catrina, right?" She gulped hard, trying to keep her composure, feeling the desire to outwardly confirm this dreaded truth.

The two boys stared at her for a moment, worried Meghan might lose it, and true enough, saying it aloud felt like sentencing Colin and Catrina to certain death.

"It does seem the most likely scenario," Ivan finally agreed. "The truth isn't so pretty, is it?" his question appeared aimed toward Jae.

A hint of hatred flitted through Jae's eyes and then disappeared.

"I handed my brother right over to her. I completely fell for the 'I'm just a poor girl in danger routine,'" Meghan mumbled.

"Try to think of it this way Meghan," Ivan said. "If they had still been here, they would very likely both be dead at this point. Besides, all three of us are to blame."

"That is true," admitted Jae. "We all knew about Catrina."

"But Colin is *my* brother. I should have been looking out for him. Now it might be too late."

"He is still alive," Ivan reminded.

"I suppose that fact will have to suffice for now," she succumbed. "I will find him, somehow... before she turns really dangerous and I lose him forever."

Jae touched her shoulder, nodded and then walked back into the meadow, helping to assist in the ongoing rescue of the imprisoned Svoda.

"Meghan," said Ivan, stopping her from following.

She turned to face him.

He stepped forward, stopping just inches from her.

"I don't mean to be ..." he stopped, searching for the right words.

"Mean? Rude? A royal pain?" Meghan answered, but with tired animosity.

"More or less," he replied, huffing slightly. "I don't... hate you," he added.

"Gee thanks," she retorted, readying another witty retort.

He put his hand over her mouth. "Will you just shut up for a minute!" He took his hand away and regained his composure. "You are so... infuriating."

Meghan held her tongue.

"I do... feel things..." he eventually spoke, but then did not finish and looked to be reprimanding himself, for being unable to formalize what he was trying to say.

Meghan said it for him.

"But you don't want to. I get it Ivan. I have no idea what you're all about. What you're up to. Or what you want from me. But I know that you cut yourself off from feeling anything real. I'm not as daft as you think."

"That's what I'm trying to say," he said, lifting his head. "Not using those exact words, however."

Meghan rolled her eyes and folded her arms.

"We don't have to be friends, Ivan. Don't worry. I won't be responsible for making you care about something." She turned to walk away once again.

He grabbed her.

She looked down at his hand, tightly gripping her arm, and then into his eyes, filled with conflict.

Behind Ivan, in the darkness of the forest, a small flame sparked to life out of nowhere.

Meghan's vision was instant.

She stood atop a hillside, watching a terrible scene erupt around her. She watched, terrified, as she picked up a knife and stabbed Catrina Flummer, and then her brother, killing them both.

It took a moment to realize that the vision had ended, as within the vision, as well as in real life, it was Ivan that held her tight, as she sobbed uncontrollably.

"What is it?" he asked, trembling. "What did you see?"

"I have to save him, Ivan. She's going to destroy him. And if I can't... I kill them both... and you help me do it!"

Ivan let go and backed away. Meghan's legs gave out and she fell to her knees, searching into the darkness for the source of the flame. All she saw now was darkness.

"No!" Ivan said emphatically. "This can't be right," he stuttered. "I would never ask you to kill your own brother. I know what I must sacrifice, but I would never..." he stepped farther back.

"I don't know what you mean, Ivan," sobbed Meghan, wishing greatly that something, anything, would make sense.

"I... forget it!" He assisted her off the ground. "Get yourself together. We should return to the group," Ivan's icy voice sent a chill down Meghan's spine.

Again, however, he was right.

There was absolutely nothing Meghan could do at this very moment, to fix the frightening future she had just witnessed. Right now, she needed to worry about what was going to happen in the next few minutes and hours.

She had broken many rules.

She had kept secrets from Juliska Blackwell.

Jae was in some kind of serious trouble and Ivan ... she still did not know what to make of Ivan.

I am fourteen and a half years old! I should be getting lost in daydreams and flipping through fashion magazines. Instead, I'm apparently plotting to kill my brother and his girlfriend!

Meghan stalked passed Ivan and into the brightly lit meadow. The pyres were now emptied and being dismantled.

She saw Juliska speaking with the Viancourt members from both groups. Surprisingly, Jae stood close by, as if waiting to speak with her. She tried to catch his eye but he ignored her.

The imprisoned Svoda seemed to be coming around and reunions with family and friends momentarily grasped their attention.

Ivan took off in the opposite direction, leaving Meghan alone. She did not try to stop him.

Meghan sighed, feeling empty, numb and tired; so tired, that she wished she could no longer feel anything.

"Maybe I can turn it off, like Ivan," she muttered. It would be much easier than feeling angry, empty and confused all the time. "But he does care... about something," she admitted. "Even Ivan cannot turn it off completely."

She whirled around, startled, after hearing the snap of a branch in the woods behind her. Her eyes darted between the trees looking for the culprit. She saw nothing, and shook it off as nerves and headed quickly into the meadow.

Behind where she had been standing, a silhouette emerged from the shadows.

"Its not the right time," Sebastien Jendaya spoke softly. "Soon, Meghan. I promise." He slipped away in the darkness.

Juliska motioned for Meghan to join her. "I need a few private words with you, please."

Meghan was surprised that Juliska did not sound angry when she spoke. The Viancourt had left to attend to other duties. Jae stayed behind, however. He nodded in a manner that told her everything would be okay.

"First, Meghan, I must apologize for my rash and unbecoming behavior earlier tonight. Being a leader requires certain choices that I am often *not* fond of making. Nevertheless, you were very brave in coming to me. The more time I have had to think on it, I realize that turning in one's brother is just about the most difficult thing one could ever do. I also see the reasoning behind keeping your silence, as discovering what appears to be an innocent girl in trouble, would garner the same decision on almost anyone's part."

Meghan once again nearly choked up. This was too much. Not even Juliska was going to be angry with her. She had betrayed her own brother... didn't she deserve some sort of punishment for her actions?

"You did not know," Juliska continued. "I'm sure you believed you were doing the right thing, in keeping your brother's secret." She leaned forward, closer to Meghan's face, becoming much more serious. "I also expect, in the future, that if anything of this sort *ever* happens again, you will tell me immediately. You are my apprentice, Meghan. And if you wish to remain so, I must know that I can trust you, completely."

She stood back up.

Meghan did not dare breathe.

"Now, I have a mess to clean up. Do not contradict *anything* that I am about to say, understood?" her voice now held a cold edge.

"Yes," Meghan replied quietly. "I'm sorry, "she added. "It will never happen again."

"Very well. We shall speak no more of it," Juliska spoke. "We have much more pressing issues at hand."

What Meghan heard intimated in Juliska Blackwell's words, was that this would be the first, and last, time she would ever clean up a mess that Meghan Jacoby had any connection to. This was strikes one, two and three. Any other missteps and she was out! Meghan did not know what *out* meant in this world, but she did not wish to be the target of Juliska's wrath.

Moreover, in truth, Meghan felt that Juliska had every right to be angry. She had hidden Catrina Flummer, after Juliska had attempted to leave the girl sleeping in a cave. Surely, this would have been a better fate. Now, because Meghan had not come forward sooner, she had unleashed a great evil into the world, and worse, that evil had attached itself to her brother.

Meghan felt shame only in that she had not come forward sooner. *At least Colin would have been free of her! He would still never forgive me, but at least he would still have a chance at a life. Now...*

Juliska Nandalia Blackwell, Banon of the Svoda Gypsies, asked for everyone's attention. The group had doubled in size, now standing at about four hundred strong.

"First, let me just acknowledge that you all have many questions and concerns. I will explain, as much as I know..." she paused as the crowd listened intently.

"Upon my group's arrival in Eidolon's Valley, I discovered a message. It held devastating news... one of the previous group's children had been deemed a Projector."

Horrified gasps, followed by a hundred questions flew at Juliska. She ignored them all and continued.

"They had advised me that a very courageous man from their caravan offered to put the girl into a deep sleep. One she should never have awakened from. He would then take her deep in the caves of Eidolon, the Goblin King, storing her body in a glass coffin, which would allow her to simply sleep away her life, living in her dreams. At the time, this seemed a better fate than killing the girl, whom they all loved dearly." Juliska's bereaved gaze turned to the Flummer family.

The crowd grew quiet, contemplating what she spoke.

Meghan noted Billie Sadorus eyeing the Flummer family. They clearly did not believe what Juliska was saying.

"Those of you in my group will recall the Initiation task I asked of Ivan Crane, to venture into the valley, seeking out a man believed held prisoner. The man of which I spoke was none other than the courageous man that tempted fate, and was so cruelly murdered at the hands of the Goblin King." She then went on to clarify, to the new group members, so they better understood what had occurred. She even retold the tale of the battle that had ended with Colin Jacoby killing a Scratcher, and reminding everyone in her group how they'd questioned how he'd accomplished such a feat.

"I believe I now know how Colin Jacoby did this incredible thing. I believe that he had the help of the Projector, at that moment. For you see, the foolish Mr. Jacoby followed our Initiate and his Learner Companion into the valley. He just could not bear to be left behind while his sister fulfilled her duties. While this was understandable at the time, it has come to my attention just earlier today, that Mr. Jacoby discovered this girl, Catrina Flummer, asleep in her coffin. And when he opened the coffin, her sleeping spell was lifted and he brought her back with him."

More stunned gasps and cries drowned out more questions that the Banon ignored.

"This cunning girl led him to believe that she was in danger and needed his help. He hid her. Kept her secret. Even from his own sister..." Juliska's tone implored her people to comprehend such a vile act.

"This girl, she cannot help it. It is her nature," Juliska added.

Meghan looked at Ivan and Jae. They each knew this was not the true story. They had all known about Catrina, a fact she assumed the Banon still did not know.

Juliska continued. "I learned all of this, as I said, earlier today, just minutes before we sounded the alarm. And how, you will ask, did I learn of this? From a brave, brave young woman that stepped forward once she discovered this girl."

"Who?" someone shouted.

"Meghan Jacoby," Juliska spoke evenly. "Meghan, you see, had a vision about this girl and confronted her brother. He lied. Told her she was wrong. There was no such girl! But she persisted and discovered the truth. And once she did, confided in me. She could see instantly that this girl was dangerous and feared for her brother's life."

Meghan had difficulty listening to Juliska speak. She understood that Juliska needed to keep the people calm, and was trying to cover for her stupidity, but she felt like Colin and Catrina were now wanted fugitives, guilty of some terrible crime. When the only thing they had ever actually done, was kill a Scratcher and fall in love...

"It was in chase of Colin Jacoby and Catrina Flummer that led us to this meadow, to our imprisoned friends and family. During which, we discovered that our enemies have some new weapon that drains our magic." Juliska then did something Meghan did not expect. She grasped Meghan's shoulders and pushed her in front of her so everyone could see.

"This brave girl not only confided about this Projector, but today, realized that this weapon did not affect her own Firemancer's abilities. Something, I, as your leader, did not recognize at the time. It was she that doused the flames that nearly burned our loved ones."

Eyes lit up in gratitude towards Meghan as Juliska announced this heroic deed. It took every ounce of strength Meghan had not to just crumble, and rather put on a generous and humble smile.

Jae grinned. This is what he had told Juliska...

Juliska allowed Meghan to step back.

She did more than step back. She took the opportunity to slip into the crowd as Juliska continued speaking.

"Most of you know the outcome of the earlier events of today. Colin Jacoby and Catrina Flummer figured out some way to escape... no doubt using her prowess as a Projector. However, because of their escape, we happened upon another discovery. One that will answer the next question I know is on all your minds."

While she paused from speaking, Meghan hid at the back of the crowd. She saw Ivan up ahead, his head tilted, noticing her standing there. He slid back, standing next to her, Meghan thought, to question Juliska's story.

"Don't Ivan," she begged. "I can't."

He nodded that he understood and for once, did not push for answers.

Meghan could not express, in words, how she felt. A shiver came over her, chilling through to her bones. Something about this entire situation just wasn't right. Her gut instinct told her this, and it was rarely incorrect.

Juliska started speaking again, but Meghan did not hear her, as Ivan then did the most unlikely of things: he put his arm around Meghan's shoulders, steadying her. She felt instantly that this was not because he liked her, or that he cared about her, but that he simply understood she needed someone to stand by her side, just for this moment. She leaned into him, trembling.

"I don't understand what I'm feeling right now, Ivan."

She realized that what she'd said probably did not make any sense.

Ivan took a deep breath, turning his head just slightly toward her.

"That's because you're beginning to understand *who* you should truly be afraid of, Meghan. And the truth…"

"Is not pretty," she breathed out.

Meghan noticed Ivan's gaze turn elsewhere. It was the girl, Maria. Her eyes flitted delicately, briefly grazing him, and then back towards Juliska.

"You like her, don't you," Meghan asked.

His gaze turned back to Meghan. "You're much more observant that I give you credit for…" he told her, reaffirming his grip firmly around her shoulders, as Juliska Blackwell regained their attention.

"I understand that all of you want to know what happens next. I don't have all the answers. We will have to figure out these things, together. The question has arisen on whether we will go our separate ways, back into our groups and continue as we were, or whether we should join as one group. My answer to this question is *neither.*"

The crowd listened intently, wondering what other possibility there could be.

"We have discovered a doorway, not previously known or documented in the Book of Doorways."

"Where does this doorway lead?" a voice called out.

When Juliska answered the crowd inhaled simultaneously, and Meghan Jacoby felt as though she might faint. Was it possible this one thing could go right?

"This door, my friends," Juliska announced, "will take us home. We are returning to our island."

##
##

If you enjoyed this book, please leave a review. Reviews help authors *a ton,* when it comes to rankings and such on Amazon.

Did you know when you buy a book via Amazon you can get the Kindle version at a huge discount? If you finish this book and decide you'd like a Kindle copy, please revisit the Amazon page for this book and your discount will be automatically given.

To read more books in this series please visit:
www.racheldaigle.com

While there, be sure to sign up for New Book Release Alerts & News Updates. Not only will you be the first to know about exciting news and book releases, but you'll get FREE side stories, cut scenes and previews from each series.

Made in the USA
Lexington, KY
06 October 2015